# Taming The Billionaire

Erica Frost

Published by Erica Frost, 2023.

TAMING THE BILLIONAIRE

**First edition. April 24, 2023.**

Copyright © 2023 Erica Frost.

ISBN: 979-8223690016

Written by Erica Frost.

# Table of Contents

# Taming the Billionaire
## New Adult Opposites Attract Romance

**By: Erica Frost**

# Foreword

A rebellious billionaire has the cash...but without the girl he resents, he'll lose it all.

Life is different now that I'm the CEO of a billion-dollar company—while the rest of the Malibu elite turn their nose down at my tattoos and dark past, I'm stuck with my new assistant trying to learn how to woo them into supporting my business and charity. But I don't trust her...especially since she grew up as rich and spoiled as the rest of them. Against my wishes, she teaches me how to blend in among the upper class. Though she's gorgeous, smart, and alluring, I have to resist the hold she has on me—I've never changed for anyone, and I'm not about to start now. And when we find ourselves posing as a couple for publicity, I know that everything she says is fake—right? This couldn't be love...could it?

# Taming The Billionaire

# Chapter One

Alec

"The event was a disaster, Alec."

These aren't the first words that I expected my assistant to say to me when I stepped into the office that fateful morning, but it's the way she greets me. I don't know why I'm surprised—after years of working together, Megan Reinhardt has made it her life's goal to call me out on everything I do, down to the type of bagel I choose for breakfast. Megan stands in the doorway of my office and blocks the entrance with her body, an eyebrow raised, a frown tugging down the corners of her lips. I cross my arms over my chest and challenge her with a grimace of my own.

"Let me into my office, Megan."

Megan sighs. She has this way of making you feel guilty with every expression that crosses her face—I hired her for public relations and marketing when Sound Connections first started to take off and become a multi-million-dollar business. And she's good at her job, don't get me wrong. But she's also a pain in my ass.

She steps out of the way and I push into my office, dropping my bag on the floor beside my desk and shrugging out of my jacket, revealing the intricate lines of tattoos along my bare forearms. Megan eyes me suspiciously.

"Casual Friday is every day now, huh?" She says, mostly joking though I can hear the distaste in her tone. "You really need to look more professional at work, Alec, or no one is ever going to take you seriously, no matter how much money you make."

"Thanks for the advice," I answer. I focus my gaze on my computer and scan over the list of waiting emails. I can feel Megan's eyes nearly burning a hole through me. "Can I help you with something else, or am I allowed to start doing some real work?"

Megan sighs and crosses the room, taking a seat in the chair across from my desk. She leans back in the chair and eyes me with suspicion. "What did I tell you to do before last night's charity event for Sound Connections?"

"You told me not to be myself," I say, rolling my eyes.

"No, I told you to not screw it up," she sighs.

"Same thing."

"I'm not trying to erase who you are, Alec, I'm just trying to present a clear and trustworthy image for the company. People are snobs and they're going to judge you for the whole," she pauses, gesturing to my tattoos, my strong arms, the glaring frown on my face, "you know, bad boy look. Listen, I know that you're a great guy."

"Really sounds like it," I respond.

"I do, Alec, I just know how people in Malibu are. They want white smiles and blonde hair and beautiful clothes. They don't want someone who's going to make them think. They want to have an easy conversation where you tell them how great they look. They don't want to see a man who looks like he'll tear their head off for fun."

"Who says I won't?" When she glares harder at me, I sigh. "It's a joke, Meg."

"See, that's what I'm talking about. I know it's a joke, but interviewers and donors don't. We're hosting these dinners and charity events under the Sound Connections brand because the company is booming and I know you want to do some good in the world with the money you're making, but no one is going to support your cause when you scare the shit out of them." Her face softens slightly, and she leans forward. "Do you see what I mean?"

"Got it, these Malibu snobs are tired of spending time with Frankenstein's monster," I answer with sharp sarcasm.

Megan rolls her eyes. "Sure, that's exactly it. Listen Alec...I think you need some help."

Sound Connections is my company through and through—I built the app from the ground up, coming up with the concept, finding and hiring the developers, funding the whole project with years of bartending work. It started with a love for music. My friends and I would work all night and put together playlists for the bar, collections of songs that we loved, that we'd spent late hours trying to learn on guitars and keyboard and basses. It was how I found my people. My best relationships were with some of the people who would come up to me and ask about what song was playing, a smile on their face, light in their eyes. I'd tell them the artist, and when they asked who made the playlist, I'd tell them it was me.

I started to think about the relationships we build through commonality—how something as simple as a song can kick off a lifetime of friendship, or even in some cases, love. So, Sound Connections was born, a dating app that connects people based on the number of songs that match on their playlists. And to my surprise, it boomed. We had over 500,000 users within the first six months. I went from washing dishes behind the bar to a billionaire in a year.

But throughout it all, I stayed who I had always been; Alec Lynch, resident asshole with a penchant for one-night stands and loud music. The money didn't change me. What it did change was the crowd that surrounded me, and I resented the rich elite that came along with a high-class Malibu lifestyle. There were days when I missed how it used to be, kicking beer cans around with my best friend Chase behind a music venue and strumming a Metallica song on his dad's guitar.

"I don't need help from anyone," I said to Megan, and I watched her face fall.

It was the truth—I'd always done my work on my own. I always would. I didn't need anyone else to tell me that I was living my life wrong. I spent years hearing it from my parents, from teachers, from ex-girlfriends. I chose my path, and I wasn't ashamed of it, and if the wealthy Malibu households didn't like the way I worked, spoke, or dressed, that was on them.

"You need to learn how to carry yourself in public. Sound Connections is doing amazing things for charity, especially for underprivileged kids in music, but it's not going to matter if people are terrified of you. Trust me, I've done the research—it's my job, Alec."

"So what, you want to get me a babysitter?"

Megan grinned. "Not a babysitter. A new kind of assistant—someone who can help show you the best way to carry yourself at these events, who knows how to schmooze her way to the top."

"Her?" I ask, eyebrow raised. "Sounds like you already have someone in mind."

Megan stands up, hands clasped in front of her. "I might have...already hired someone."

"Megan," I groan, running a hand down my face in exasperation, "I did not give approval for that kind of thing."

She smiles sheepishly. "I know, I know, I'm sorry, better to ask for forgiveness than permission, right? I promise you it will be worth it—Thalia is a gem. She's smart, clever, hardworking, dedicated, and she loves Sound Connections. You're going to be thanking me, I swear."

Megan makes her way over to the door and holds a hand out in front of her, beckoning for me to follow. "Come on, humor me. Want to meet her?"

In fact, meeting anyone new was the last thing I had in mind, especially not a new employee that I didn't approve of. But I like Megan, and by now she's become almost a member of this makeshift family I've built over the years—if she truly thinks this is for the better, maybe I have to trust her.

"Fine," I say with a huff, pushing away from my desk. I follow her out into the hallway, and as soon as I step past the door I—

Get knocked onto my back by a speeding force. I let out a surprised shout, hitting the wood floor hard with an oof, the breath stolen from my chest.

"Oh my god, I'm so sorry, I'm sorry, I didn't mean to, I wasn't looking where I was going and I—oh my god, you're Alec, I mean Mr. Lynch, again I'm so so sorry—"

I look into the eyes of a beautiful girl. Her gaze is wide and honey brown and anguished as she hovers over me, her hands pressing into my chest, her blonde hair falling around us in a curtain that smells of vanilla and flowers.

"Get off," I grunt.

The girl scrambles back and gets to her feet. She extends one hand as an offer to help me up while brushing off her pencil skirt with the other, her ankles wobbling in ridiculously high heels. While I have to admit that they make her legs look incredible, I resent them immediately for sending her tumbling down on top of me. I ignore her offered hand and get to my feet, straightening my shirt. Megan stands beside us, a horrified hand pinned over her mouth.

"I'm sorry," the girl says again, sheepish, her cheeks pink. "I thought I was late so I was in a rush but I guess—it turns out—I was actually on time." She smiles now, but her eyes are still panicked. "That one is on me."

Megan clears her throat. "Alec, this is Thalia Weaver, your new assistant who will be taking over some of my work and helping to educate you on the proper etiquette you'll need for interviews, dinners, and charity events." She shoots Thalia a scathing glance. "I promise, she's better at it than she looks."

Thalia gives me an embarrassed grin and holds her hand out again. "It's a pleasure to meet you, sir."

I stare at her hand and cross my own over my chest. She hesitates for a moment before dropping it down by her side again, then pinning it behind her back.

"I don't need help," I say again, "especially not from a clumsy kid."

Thalia's eyes narrow. "I'm not a kid, sir, and I'm willing to bet that I have more industry experience than some of the professionals you've worked with in the past. I might still be working toward my undergraduate degree, but I've spent my life interacting with people in the sphere that your business exists in, and I know how capable I am of proving myself."

Megan grins. "See, I told you that she was good."

I turn away from both of them and head back into my office. "I don't care what the two of you want to do," I call over my shoulder. I sit down at my computer and try to focus on my work again. "Just leave me out of whatever mess you create."

Thalia appears in my doorway, a hand propped on her hip. She looks like a dream in the creamy blouse and dark skirt that hug her curves. Her chin is high, her eyes dark and focused, and her mouth is set in a sure smirk.

"You won't regret having me on your side, Mr. Lynch. In fact, I think you'll be thanking me sooner than you expect."

"Whatever you say," I answer with a scoff. "Shut the door behind you."

She watches me for a moment before I look up and fix her with a levelled glare. "Did you hear me?" I ask gruffly.

"Loud and clear, sir," she answers with a pleasant smile. "I'm looking forward to working with you."

I don't dignify her words with a response. But when she closes the door with an echoing click, I find that I can still feel the heat of her gaze on my cheek, and the firm pressure of her body pressed against mine.

What has Megan gotten me into this time?

# Chapter Two

Thalia

After all the hours I spent preparing my resume, interviewing, and talking myself out of my anxieties, I had expected my first day on the job to go a little differently. I'll be the first to admit it—running into my new boss and knocking the two of us onto the ground wasn't exactly my idea of a great first impression.

My mother always raised me to present myself professionally. Growing up under her strict doctoral sensibilities and my father's political work, there was never an opportunity to let my guard down. It was always chin up, Thalia. Pull yourself together, Thalia. Smile, Thalia.

So, I did. It came naturally to me, and my parents loved to parade me around as their prized child. Even when I realized that this was not the life I wanted, that I'd rather stray from the path they had carved out for me, I stuck to the script, because it was easier and I liked to feel like they were proud of me.

It seemed to please Megan when I showed up to our interview appointment dressed to the nines and ready to schmooze. She's a smart woman—I knew it from the moment our eyes locked, and she asked me how I felt about my father's political work. He's known around Malibu for his recent campaign for mayor, so it's not a surprise that Megan would hear the name Thalia Weaver and put the pieces together.

"I'm proud of my father and the work that he does," I had said, my legs crossed and my hands folded in my lap. "But it's not a world that I see myself being a part of. I'm more interested in the philanthropic work that Sound Connections presents, and I'd like to put my skills to better use by contributing to that cause."

Megan had smiled then, a genuine thing, and it lit something up inside of me—hope, hope that maybe this would be my moment, my chance to prove to myself and my family that just because I didn't have a desire to be a doctor or to involve myself in politics didn't mean that I was a disaster.

"I think you'll be a great addition to the Sound Connections team. I'm warning you now, Alec won't like it—he thinks he's perfect when it comes to interacting with donors and potential business partners. But he's intimidating, and he can be a little bit of a dick. Just don't tell him I said that."

"Your secret's safe with me," I had promised.

So I got the job. And in a matter of minutes, I plowed down my new boss, knocking him flat on his back and landing on top of him like an idiot.

But maybe, if I'm lucky, first impressions are a myth—maybe today can be my fresh start. My first real day of work under Alec's leadership, learning from someone completely removed from the Malibu elite that I grew up around. It's a chance for me to learn how to prove myself, and for me to truly make a difference.

I pick out a dress for the day, a curve-hugging number that I know makes me look good but falls just below my knees, professional and clean cut. I curl my hair until it falls in loose blonde waves and add just a touch of makeup—some concealer under my eyes to hide the dark circles earned from late night thesis sessions, some blush along my cheekbones to wake me up. When I look in the mirror before heading out the door, sensible heels strapped on and keys in hand, I feel capable and sure of myself. There's no way this day could be anything but good.

I drive over to the Sound Connections office. Megan gave me a part time position—I still have class most mornings to finish up my senior year at Santa Monica College, until I'll earn my communications degree. But now my afternoons are devoted to Sound Connections and the career that I'll hopefully build there.

The sun is high in the sky as I park my car and head into the building. Megan told me to report to Alec's office at noon, so I climb the stairs and try to level my breathing before finding his door and knocking three times. My heart hums in my chest as I wait for his response.

"Come in," Alec says, voice low and casual. I swing the door open and give him a winning smile.

"Oh, it's you," he says when his eyes land on me. There's a suspicious glint in his gaze, with a twist of his mouth that tells me he's not too thrilled to see me standing in his doorway.

"Good afternoon," I answer crisply. "Can I come in?"

His eyes narrow. "Um, I suppose. Did Megan tell you to come bother me?"

I try not to let my smile falter, though annoyance peaks in my mind. Megan did warn me that Alec would be hesitant to accept my help, and after yesterday's greeting, I don't quite know what else I expected. But I'm here to do a job and I plan on doing it well. I'm not going to let a man—albeit a gorgeous, successful one—tear me down.

Alec looks entirely intimidating behind his desk. He's dressed casually in a t-shirt and slacks. The dark t-shirt shows off his heavily tattooed arms, intricate illustrations lining his arms in the form of snakes, flames, and scripted words. His hair is slicked back, a dark coif that makes him look timeless and handsome, and the afternoon sun streaming through his windows illuminates his defined jawline. I clear my throat and straighten my spine.

"Actually, Megan informed me that she'd be meeting us both in your office at 12:15."

Alec peers at me suspiciously and takes a glance at his watch. At that exact moment, Megan glides in, her short hair gelled back and a brilliant smile wide on her face.

"Hello everyone, glad we could gather here today," she says breezily, taking a seat across from Alec's desk. She gestures to the chair beside her and urges me to sit. I do so after a moment of hesitation. Alec looks positively furious.

"Why are we doing this in my office, Meg?" He asks, looking pained. "I have real work that needs to be done."

"This is real work, my dear." She snaps open a notepad and starts to make furious notes. Alec and I wait in silence. I fidget in my chair.

"So, as your PR manager, it's my job to make sure that Sound Connections is surrounded by good press. We want to pull people in with the media that we share."

"I know this already," Alec snaps.

"Patience, please," Megan says, and I get the feeling that not many people feel free enough to speak like this around Alec. He rolls his eyes at her tone and steeples his fingers in front of his face.

"Just get to the point please."

"Right on," Megan says quickly. "The point is—you two are a couple now."

"Excuse me?" I ask, face going hot, as Alec's face falls into slack shock.

"What the hell are you talking about?" He asks, voice low and tense.

"Sound Connections is first and foremost a dating app," Megan says. "People want to believe in love, and they want to believe that they could find their perfect person somewhere out there. But our studies show that people want evidence—they want to see someone out there who used Sound Connections and fell in love along the way."

"So why does that mean we're a couple?" I ask, my voice high and tense with sudden nerves. Alec won't look in my direction, and I find myself grateful that I don't have to feel the weight of his gaze on me.

"Alec is the spokesperson for the company," Megan says. "He created it. It's his baby, and that means people look to him for representation. If they could see that he fell in love through his own app, it would show that he's relatable, down to earth, and would quite frankly make him more approachable than he currently is."

"Can you explain this without insulting me?" Alec grits out.

"Sorry, but it's the truth. We need a new vision for the company that advertises the truth of falling in love, and we need two hot people like yourselves to show it off."

"But it's a lie," I say bluntly before I realize what I'm doing. "How are we supposed to make people believe in that?"

Megan shrugs. "You're two hot people in your prime. People will believe anything if we make it convincing enough."

"No way," Alec says, shaking his head. "I have much more important work to do. I'm not playing boyfriend when I need to be organizing funds, keeping the app running, finding donors for our charity work. This is ridiculous."

"This is how you find those donors, Alec," Megan insists, hands waving as she talks. "People thrive on a good love story. Trust me on this, okay? It's my job."

Alec shakes his head again but doesn't answer. I feel like my world is spinning. Pretend to date Alec Lynch? On the first day of my new job? This isn't exactly what I thought I'd be signing up for—I thought I'd be behind the scenes, helping him adjust to the reality of rich Malibu society, reeling in donors for the Sound Connections Foundation and raising money for underprivileged kids in the area.

"You won't regret it," Megan says, and by the way Alec sighs I get the sense that this is something she's said to him before.

"Just tell me what I need to do," he answers, leaning back in his chair. His eyes flicker over to me for a split second. I feel the heat in them as they land on me, a mix of resentment and curiosity that burns down through my stomach. I hold his gaze, challenging him to look away, but neither of us will give up on this game.

When I finally break our eye contact and turn to Megan, my cheeks flushed, she has a sly grin on her face. "You'll make your first public appearance as a couple at Sound Connections' next event," she says. "It's next Friday evening. It's a dinner event, with tons of local potential donors and elite members of Hollywood. You'll both need to be on your best behavior. If we can pull it off, people will fall in love with your story, and they'll be begging to get involved. In the meantime, this is where you get to work, Thalia. I need you to show Alec the ropes—he needs to be ready to wine and dine these people without acting like a fool."

Alec flips her off. Megan smiles sweetly.

"Then that's that," she says, "I'll be in touch."

She slips out of the office without another word and I'm left there in the other chair, staring dumbly at Alec, unsure of what my next move will be.

"Well, um, since I'm here, is there anything that you need from me, Mr. Lynch?"

Alec leans back in his chair and levels me with a gaze. "I need for you to leave, so I can get my work done."

I nod slowly and give him a smile full of disdain. "As you wish, sir. I'll see myself out."

I get up, gathering my things and preparing to leave. "Wait, Thalia," Alec says, and I turn back to face him, thinking that maybe he'll apologize for being rude. But instead, he just holds out an envelope.

"Drop this at the post office for me, will you?"

"Of course," I say flatly, and I snatch the envelope from his hands, leaving the office without another word.

Maybe this job was a mistake, I think as I walk back through the halls and toward my car, cursing Alec Lynch's name with every step.

Oh well. I'm already in too deep. Might as well dive in, head first.

# Chapter Three

Alec

"You have a lunch reservation at 12:30," Megan says as I step into the office the next morning. I've barely taken a sip from my coffee before she shoves a piece of paper into my hands. "You'll meet Thalia there. You'll eat together, and you'll act like you're having the time of your life, and a photographer will get pictures of the two of you. They'll be all over the tabloids before you can blink."

"Huh?" I say, eloquently. I take a look at the paper in my hands. It's outlined with an itinerary of my day, and there it is in black and white—Lunch with Thalia.

"This is ridiculous," I start, but Megan has already turned and started walking away. She waves over her shoulder.

"12:30! Don't be late!"

The morning passes slowly as I work through a steady stream of emails and phone calls. I don't know why there's a bundle of nerves humming inside of me, a strange anticipation for that afternoon. The last thing I want to do is leave the office for whatever little stunt Megan has planned. While I have to admit that she's never steered me wrong in the past, I just can't wrap my head around how this fake dating situation could possibly be beneficial.

But I follow through, because if I'm anything, I'm dependable—I leave the office at noon and head downtown to the restaurant, a place with an outdoor garden called LA Bohemia.

Thalia is waiting at a table by the time I get there. Even I can admit that she looks lovely—the sun glints off her hair, illuminating her face, and the casual dress that she's chosen is light and airy and perfect for the spring weather. I take the seat across from her and the surprised look she gives me is sweet, innocent almost. But I'm not here to play to the whims of a college girl who's coasting by on her parents' money. I'm doing this because I trust Megan, so I have to see her project through—even if it drives me crazy in the process.

"Good to see you, Mr. Lynch," Thalia says, smiling demurely.

"Call me Alec," I correct. "If we're really going to be seen in public as a couple, then it's going to sound incredibly awkward if you're calling me Mr. Lynch. Besides, it makes me feel old."

Thalia's smile falters but manages to cling to her face. "Okay, well, fine, Alec it is then." She circles a hand around a sweating glass of water and looks at it like it might save her from this uncomfortable situation. "Though who knows," she says, tone mocking, "maybe we're just into that whole thing, Mr. Lynch the professional."

I roll my eyes. "No thank you, I'd rather not find my name printed in some headline that declares an assumption about my behavior in the bedroom."

Thalia's cheeks flush and I look away, feeling embarrassment creep into my own expression.

"Well, what do you want to read about yourself in the tabloids then?" Thalia asks, sipping her water.

I shrug. "I'd rather not be involved. But I know it's necessary to keep the business running and our charity funded, so I do what I need to do."

Thalia nods slowly as a waitress comes over to take our orders. Thalia picks out a strawberry salad, and I settle for a sandwich that doesn't sound particularly appetizing. I cross my arms over my chest as she walks away again.

"Don't look so excited to be here," Thalia says, raising an eyebrow. "People are going to think that our first date was spent berating each other."

"It's not a date," I snap, instinctually. Thalia narrows her eyes at me, but the smile never slips from her lips. Somehow, it feels like a challenge.

"Well, of course I know that, but whoever Megan decided to tip off isn't going to assume that we're staging this mess."

Thalia crosses her legs. She's everything that I swore I'd stay away from, growing up. She carries her upbringing in the way she sits, how she tucks her napkin into her lap, the brilliant smile she gives the waiter when he drops off our food.

She takes a bit of her food, dainty and pristine. I chew on my own food without a care for how it looks—I'm not here to impress anyone, especially not here, and I'm not about to pretend like I am. I'll put up with this mess if it makes Megan happy, but I'm not going to change who I am for a publicity stunt.

"While we're here, I might as well learn a few things about who you are," Thalia says, politely swallowing behind a manicured hand.

"I'm the CEO of Sound Connections."

It looks like it takes everything in her not to roll her eyes, a fact that gives me a twinge of satisfaction. I can't hold back my own smirk.

"Good one. Tell me something real." She flushes, clearly questioning if she should be speaking to me like that, and I'm tempted to call her out for treating me like a friend and not a boss. But it's kind of refreshing to hear, especially from someone like her who clearly has spent her whole life with a stick up her ass.

"I grew up in Malibu."

Thalia looks surprised.

"I know, hard to believe," I continue, "but the city isn't all rich people like the ones you're used to."

"I didn't say that," Thalia says, eyes wide. "I just—I wasn't expecting, you know, the way you are when you're in spaces like this. You don't seem like you like it here all that much."

I look around at the sunny patio, well-dressed people laughing and drinking and talking animatedly. I shrug. It's not that I hate Malibu itself, it's just that...

"Malibu doesn't like me," I answer. "Or at least, it doesn't like people who look like me."

Thalia's eyes trace down my arms, and I watch as she takes in my detailed tattoos and the grimace on my face. "You do stand out," she admits, and I laugh under my breath.

"That's one way to put it."

If I stand out, Thalia blends in perfectly. She looks sun-kissed, like she was raised by the ocean waves themselves, made to be a part of the city where she grew up. She has an air of money to her, clinging to her clothes and her light hair and her golden smile. I wonder what it's like to have a life like that—one where you never have to want for anything, just living your days on your own terms until you wind up settling down and having a few kids. It seems completely unrealistic and unattainable to me—like my worst fears coming to life.

A click of a shutter draws my attention back to the moment. I'm leaning back in my seat, eyes trained on Thalia as my thoughts drift away from me. She reaches across the table and takes my hand in hers and I have to fight not to jump away from her touch.

Through a clenched-teeth smile, Thalia says, "Hold my hand."

I sit up a little and tighten my fingers around hers. "This is ridiculous," I say, smiling pleasantly.

"You think I don't know that? Your hand is really sweaty, you know."

I glare at the impish smile that crosses her face before trying to school my expression into something that the cameras won't pick apart. Megan is really on my shit list for this one.

"Okay, well, it's hot out right now," I say under my breath, and Thalia laughs, tossing her head back and squeezing my hand harder. "I can't believe we're doing this."

"I can't believe you agreed to it," Thalia answers with a shrug. "Is promoting your business worth pretending to date me?"

I watch her quizzical gaze. I don't trust her—that much is clear—but I can tell that Thalia is smarter than she looks. That makes her dangerous, too.

"It's not about the business," I say. "It's more than that. It's one thing to convince people that our app works, that music really does bring people together, that it does create lasting connections. But what I'm really trying to build is our charity. I didn't exactly have the best upbringing, and my school's music program saved me, so I want to give back to the same establishments that helped me pull my life together."

Thalia's eyes trace over me, like she's sizing me up. "Wow, that's actually pretty noble of you."

I roll my eyes, hoping a camera doesn't pick that up. "Don't sound so surprised. Are we done here yet?"

Thalia takes another bite of her salad, smiling. "Not yet, honey," she says, voice sickly sweet. "We need to talk about how we're going to approach this benefit dinner that Megan mentioned. We need a plan for how we're going to make you presentable for the event."

I scoff. "Megan is delusional. I'm perfectly fine, and there's nothing that needs to be done."

Thalia raises an eyebrow. It sends a jolt of annoyance through me, and I drop her gaze.

"Come on, you and I both know that that's not exactly true or I would have never been hired."

"Exactly, and I didn't want to hire you," I snap. Thalia's face falls just a fraction, but the smile is back on her lips in seconds.

"Let's think about this. Megan told me that you're having trouble making connections at these events, and that it's difficult for you to find donors because of it."

"Not true," I say, under my breath. "You can't blame me for not wanting to suck up to people who never cared if I lived or died growing up."

Thalia smiles ruefully. "Smile, dear," she says through her teeth. "Let's try this—imagine that I'm a rich executive and you want me to make a donation."

I don't have to try hard to picture it—Thalia already looks the part. I pull my hand back from hers and cross my arms over my chest. "Done."

"How would you greet me?"

"This is a waste of time," I say, not wanting to play along with whatever this game is.

"It's so nice to meet you too," Thalia says, in a voice that's full of false cheer. "Just trust me, Alec, it's my job to help you. I'm not here to try and make your life more difficult."

But that's the issue—I don't trust her, and she is making my life more difficult. None of this stuff matters to me, it's all just a distraction from the actual end goal of building up the company and the charity until we're helping to change the world for the lives of kids like me who spent their teens trying to find somewhere to sleep and getting shady tattoos in somebody's basement or garage. Kids who sought music as an escape from uncertainty.

If I can help them, then it's all worth it, isn't it?

"Fine," I grit out. "Hi. How are you."

"A little more enthusiasm and less venom next time, but sure, that's better," Thalia says. "You have to make people think that you're comfortable with being around them, even if you're not."

"I'm not a liar," I say, and I want to finish with not like you. But I hold my tongue.

"I'm not asking you to be a liar, I'm just asking you to...pretend," she says, wincing at her own words.

"This is why I don't trust any of you people," I say bitterly. I drop a few twenties on the table and push away from it. "Can we go now?"

Thalia blinks back at me. "Um, sure, I suppose."

She gets to her feet, grabbing her bag, and with resentment burning hard inside of me, I extend a hand to her. She takes it warily. I'm sure we look positively stupid, two people wincing at the sight of their own hands intertwined. But if this is what Megan says will work, then fine. I have to go with it.

We walk back to the parking lot like that. Thalia leads me to her car first, a sleek Mercedes that fits exactly what I imagined she might drive—clean, understated, expensive. It takes everything in me not to sneer at the sight of it. I wonder if this girl has ever worked for the things she wants, or if she's used to having her parents' money to do it for her.

"Hey," I say as she turns to go, and when she glances back at me I tug her into me and press a fleeting kiss to her cheek. She flushes, eyes wide, and I plaster a smile on my face. "Let's hope that convinces them enough."

"Sure," Thalia says, and her voice almost sounds a bit shaky. I wonder if I managed to catch her off guard and I feel a little sense of satisfaction in my chest.

"See you back at the office," I say, and I turn to my car, getting behind the wheel and peeling out of the parking lot before I can overthink what I just did.

That afternoon as I'm settling back in behind my desk, Megan knocks on the door.

"Thanks for being a trooper today, Alec," she says with a bright grin. I grunt in response, my eyes trained to my screen. "The cameraman sent over some stills for me to double check, and while I can say that you do look kind of constipated, they're not half bad. They'll definitely do, in a pinch. Friday's event is going to be our best benefit yet."

When I nod in response but don't meet her eyes, she calls to me until I finally look up. "Thanks again," she says. "I promise this will be worth it. And Thalia's a talented woman—be happy I got you someone hot to flirt with." She winks and turns, leaving me alone in my office once again, scowling at the empty doorway.

# Chapter Four

Thalia

As I'm leaving my morning class the next day, my phone rings with my mom's name lighting up the screen. I sigh, clear my throat, and answer with a cheery "Hello!"

"Thalia Hope, tell me what I'm looking at right now."

I check my watch—thirty minutes to make it to the office for this afternoon's shift. It's time for another day of Alec looking at me like I'm gum stuck on the bottom of his shoe.

"I don't know Mother, you tell me what you're looking at," I answer with another sigh.

"The tabloids, dear. Care to explain why Alec Lynch is kissing you on the cheek?"

My stomach sinks. I forgot that the photos taken of us were public things. I forgot that my parents, uptight Sarah and Robert Weaver, would see and hate.

"I told you, remember? I have a new internship at Sound Connections, working with his charity. He's just being nice."

"This looks like a lot more than being nice, honey, the article is saying that the two of you are a couple!"

"You know how the tabloids are," I say, fumbling with my keys as I climb into the car. "They love to blow things out of proportion."

"I just want you to be careful, honey. You know I don't like you getting involved in this nonprofit work. You need to be focusing on a career that will build your reputation and set you up for success later in life."

My mother has always been this way: goal-oriented, focused on gains only, discovering the one thing that will set her another step forward. She passed it down to me, with her freckles and her smile to match.

"This is—this is important to me, Mother. We're going to make a difference."

She sighs on the other end of the phone, and I can already hear the argument she's about to launch into. You need to make money, Thalia. We won't support you forever, Thalia. You need to consider medicine, not communications, Thalia. You're throwing your life away, Thalia.

So what if I am? Would it really be that bad, to not be rich, to just be happy? It seems that my parents think so. I'm not as sure if I agree.

Money is great, sure. It's easy for me to say that when I've had it my whole life. But all this time, all these years, I don't think I've ever seen my parents truly happy. Their lives have always been about pleasing others and presenting a curated image of themselves to the public. That's not a life I want for myself.

"You need to be conscious of your presence in public," my mother says at last. "Things like this...they'll affect your father's campaign. I wish you'd just come work for his office instead."

I wrinkle my nose as I pull my car out of the campus parking lot and start heading to the Sound Connections office. "Listen, Mother, I'm sorry but I have to go. Work is about to start. I'll see you for dinner next weekend though, okay? I love you."

"Love you too, dear," she answers, before I hang up. It takes everything in me not to let my forehead fall forward and press on the horn. It's barely noon and I'm already exhausted.

I park at the office and hurry up the stairs in my unsteady heels, barely making it inside before the clock strikes 12.

"Thalia!" Megan says with delight as soon as I step into the office. She's standing near her desk, a cell phone pressed to her ear. She waves me over. "I'm so glad you're here. Alec has a fitting in thirty minutes for a new suit, and I need you to go with him. Last time he just got one from Macy's. Macy's! The man is a billionaire and doesn't know how to dress himself, it's truly sad."

Whoever is on the other end of the phone must be speaking now, because Megan says, "No, no, not you. I said we need a seating chart for Friday, okay?"

She waves me in the direction of Alec's office, so I nod quickly and head over to his cracked door. I knock twice before entering and shutting the door behind me.

He looks up, surprised by my entry. "Hello," I say, feeling suddenly nervous with his eyes on me, studying.

"Can I help you?"

"I think I'm the one who's supposed to be asking that question," I answer. Alec scoffs, thumbing through a stack of papers and finally taking his judgement filled eyes off me. "Megan said you have a suit fitting. We should probably leave now, if we want to make it on time."

Alec shakes his head. "I'm not going to that. I have a perfectly fine suit that I can wear."

I eye his black t-shirt and slacks with suspicion. "She said we had to."

"Megan says a lot, but this is my company."

I sigh, leaning back against his door. "Come on, Alec. Don't make me pretend to date a man who looks like a slob in public. I have standards, you know."

"A slob?" He repeats, incredulous. When he looks up and sees my teasing smile, he rolls his eyes. "Fine. Let me finish this and meet me at my car."

His car is exactly like him—clean, understated, dark and quiet. It's not what you'd expect a billionaire to be driving, but it's nice all the same. I feel nervous as I climb into the passenger seat, like I'm about to go on a real date. Alec rolls the windows down and turns the music up as we drive, effectively cutting off any chance of the two of us having a real conversation. No big deal. I didn't want to talk to him anyway.

The fitting is at a small, upscale boutique downtown. Alec leads the way as an attendant greets us. When he sees Alec's name, his eyes widen.

"Right this way, Mr. Lynch," he says, leading us to a private room with seats and a full-length mirror. "I have your measurements recorded here, thanks to your assistant, and I'll be right back with some options for you to try on."

The attendant leaves the room and Alec takes a seat. I sit beside him in the other chair, crossing my legs.

"This is ridiculous," he says with a groan.

"That must be your catchphrase," I joke. He flashes a glare in my direction, but the attendant returns before he can snap back at me.

"Here you are, sir. I'll give you a few moments to get changed and then we'll tailor each piece to make sure that you're getting the best possible fit." He steps out of the room again and I hurry to follow him, not having to be told to leave for Alec to strip down but also fighting the weird, small part of me that wants to stick around and see the type of muscle he's hiding under those flimsy t-shirts and dark pants.

When I come back into the room, the attendant is adjusting his cuffs and fixing the collar of the suit jacket. Alec does clean up well—he looks sleek and professional in the suit, like the billionaire I expected to find when I started working at Sound Connections. His face is blank, however, and it's impossible to tell how he feels about the suit. In fact, it feels impossible to tell what Alec is feeling, ever. He keeps everyone around him iced out, seemingly even those he trusts.

"It looks good," I say, surprising myself. Alec meets my eyes in the mirror. His gaze is hard, his mouth set in an annoyed line. The attendant flashes me a grateful smile.

"You do look great, sir," the attendant adds. "Your girlfriend is a lucky woman."

My eyes widen and I cross my arms over my chest, instantly stammering out, "Actually, you see—"

"Thank you," Alec interrupts. "You can leave us for now."

The attendant nods and leaves Alec and I to examine the suit in the mirror. "Did you forget you're supposed to be dating me?" Alec says, his voice wry and mocking.

"No, I just—I was caught off guard. I'm sorry."

Alec turns away from the mirror and ignores my apology. Why does he have to make me feel like I'm always saying the wrong thing? "This is a waste of money. I have a perfectly good suit at home."

I scoff. "Sure, if you want to look like a kid at his junior prom."

Alec scowls at me. "What would you know about the suits I already have?"

"Alec, you're not exactly flying under the radar with your company. There are pictures of you at formal events all over the internet. You look like a lost teenager in all of them."

"You're asking to get fired with a comment like that," he says, with bite in his tone.

But I can't help but push him. Something about him truly gets under my skin, encouraged by the knowledge that he needs me to reach his fundraising goals. "Sure, go ahead and fire me. But you're going to regret walking into Friday's benefit looking like a charity case."

Alec refuses to meet my eyes now, starting to shrug out of the suit jacket.

"Wait," I call out, and I fix the shoulder of the jacket, feeling a tense little spark where we touch. He starts, surprised, and trains his eyes on my cheek as I straighten the suit. "This one is good, but it doesn't flatter your waist like it has the potential to. We need to try another."

I drop my hands away from him like the jacket is on fire. He seems distracted, watching me move, his mouth pressed into a sealed line.

"Fine," he says roughly. "Make this quick."

I find the attendant at the front of the store and together we pick out two more options—a sleek dark blue number that will go perfectly with Alec's eyes, and a deep charcoal gray suit that I think he might enjoy.

"Get the blue," I tell Alec as he watches himself in the mirror, the attendant straightening the back of the jacket. I was right about the compliment to his eye color—the suit makes him look as sleek and professional as he's meant to present himself. The curling edges of his tattoos emerge at his wrists and the exposed skin of his neckline. He looks in control, masterful and cold, the same man I remember bumping into my first day at the office. He's gorgeous.

"Fine," Alec says, voice blunt and icy. "If it's what we have to do, then get it."

Gorgeous, but still an asshole.

But I consider the day a success. As we drive back to the office, the suit boxed up and ready to go for the benefit event, I can't hide the small smile that graces my face.

"Thanks for cooperating," I say. "I know you think the suit isn't necessary, but you have to trust me. I grew up going to a million of these things, and people will only respect you if you give them a reason to."

Alec doesn't turn to meet my eyes as he drives, one strong hand turning the wheel with ease, but I do see his eyebrows furrow.

"I don't trust anyone," Alec says. "Don't take it personally."

But I can't help it. I fold my hands in my lap and turn away from Alec, watching the landscape flit by, resenting him the whole ride back.

# Chapter Five

Alec

The past week has been nothing but a blur of errands that pulled me away from the real work that needs to be done. Awkward lunch dates and suit fittings are the least of my worries—there are guest lists to be made, seating arrangements, valet companies, caterers. There's the important question of how payments will be made, what school they will benefit, what kind of instruments we'll select to support the students and their interests. And then there's everything beyond Friday's event as it comes up quickly—there's the rest of the business to consider, numbers and statistics and new playlists being released every day.

I'm lucky to have employees to support me, but there are always some things that end up biting me in the ass—like hiring Megan.

"Knock knock," she says cheerily as she enters my office Wednesday morning. "How's it going boss?"

"Fine," I answer, not wanting to look up from my work because I know a little bit of eye contact is all she needs to enthusiastically assign me some other inane task.

"So, listen, we're going to need—"

"Not today, Meg, please. I have so much that needs to be done and I can't handle another useless etiquette session. We've already made progress in our last few charity events, haven't we?"

When I do meet her eyes, Megan looks doubtful. "Alec, you know I love you. I do, truly. But at our last event, you told the CEO of a rival company that you didn't care what he thought and you hoped his business tanked. And he could have donated up to a hundred thousand dollars, Alec!"

"Well," I answer bitterly. "He called me cheap."

"See, that's my point exactly. Don't give people reasons to come for you. You need to be bulletproof. So my play for you and Thalia today is—"

"To visit Malibu High," I finish. "We need to stop by the school and speak with the director to find out what instruments they need most. That we can promote it at the event."

Megan blinks a few times, surprised. "Well, that's not what I was going to suggest, but I suppose it's not the worst idea. Fine. You and Thalia head over to the school then. But I'm rescheduling your lunch time appointment to dinner—you need to learn how to eat like a civilized human being, based on the tabloid photos I saw. You were tearing into your sandwich like an animal. Thalia will give you some pointers at the Italian place across town, got it?"

I roll my eyes as Megan stalks away, her boots clicking on the floor. It's not worth fighting her on the subject. She acts as if I've been eating with my hands my whole life, animalistic and raw. But I don't care that I come off as uncouth or out of control. It's just dinner. It's just conversation. I'm just trying to be myself, and not some stuck up prick that doesn't know his own worth.

As the afternoon winds down I meet Thalia in the conference room as she scrolls through something on her laptop, eyebrows narrowed in focus. "We're going," I tell her, and she looks up in surprise.

"Going? Where? I thought dinner wasn't until later tonight."

"We have to stop by the high school that we're supporting with Friday's funds."

Thalia nods and gathers her things, following me out of the room but hanging a safe distance back from me, like I have the potential to lash out and bite her. Whatever—not my problem if she's uncomfortable around me.

We ride to the school together in my car. The roads there are so familiar—back when I was a teenager, I used to drive my beat-up truck down these same roads, looking for trouble to get into. We'd pic someone's house and hang out in the basement, drinking and listening to music and strumming on guitars. Back then all I cared about was doing whatever I wanted. I didn't want to be told anything. My parents gave up on me when I finally dropped out of high school my senior year. It wasn't that I hated learning—I was just tired of people hating me because of the way I looked, and the lack of interest I had in wasting my time in class. The only teacher who ever got that was my music teacher, Mr. Johnston. He taught me how to play the guitar and encouraged me to learn to play the songs that I loved. And when I dropped out, he took to calling me once in a while, asking how I was doing, telling me not to give up on music. I don't know where I'd be without him.

"Why Malibu High School?" Thalia had asked as soon as we got into the car. I didn't have to ask to know that she likely attended one of the pricy private schools in town, like La Salle. Our upbringings were so different—I didn't need to hear her talk about being valedictorian or prom queen to know that.

"They need our help," I answered, not wanting to reveal anymore. My past was my past. I'm not ashamed of it, not trying to hide anything, but that doesn't mean I want to suddenly open up and spill my feelings to a girl who hates my guts and likely wouldn't understand what I was trying to say anyway.

Luckily, she hadn't pushed the subject in that moment. It seemed that Thalia was learning exactly how I liked to operate. When I don't speak, it's for a reason. Hopefully she understands that and stops trying to push me where I'm not comfortable.

Malibu High looks exactly as I remember it. The afternoon sun paints the whole thing a bleary sepia tone. There are kids milling around, sitting on benches, eyeing my car suspiciously when it pulls up. I don't blame them—if I had still been a student here and I saw a nice car park out front, I would have been curious too. But when I get out of the car, casual clothes and tattoos on display, the kids seem to relax a little. They're used to a guy like me, rough around the edges, prepared to stand up for myself. It's not who they expected, but it's who they respect. Thalia, on the other hand, looks completely out of place as she climbs out of the car. Her dress is too bright, too finely tailored. Her hair shines with a sort of unattainable beauty under the hot California sun. And her cheeks are dusted with pink, her eyes wide and sweet. I expect her to turn right around and hop back into the car, intimidated by the stares the kids have trained on her. But instead, a brilliant smile works its way across her face, and she waves at a bunch of kids sitting at a picnic table with that grin aimed their way.

Uncertainly, I watch as they wave back at her, surprised but genuine in their reactions.

"Let's go," I say roughly, before clearing my throat. Thalia gives me a little look like don't rush me but I ignore it, instead urging her forward with a hand on the small of her back. She doesn't push back against my touch like I expected her to, but follows me as I asked. It's a refreshing change.

Inside the school, I'm overwhelmed with memories. The place looks exactly the same and makes me feel like a giant. The last time I was here, I was a skinny kid with only a couple stick and poke tattoos adorning my arms. Now I've bulked up after years of working out and taking care of my body, and I have professional art covering my skin. School has already let out for the day so the only kids around are the stragglers. I lead Thalia to the music room, muscle memory carrying me there before I can realize what exactly I'm doing.

Mr. Johnston gives me a warm smile when he sees me. "Alec! It's been a while. Who is this beauty you have on your arm?"

Thalia blushes and smiles, that charming look she has crossing her face. "This is Thalia, my..." I answer, trailing off. "My girlfriend."

The word feels weird in my mouth, and I hate that I have to say it. That I have to lie to Mr. Johnston who has only ever asked for the truth from me. But he looks so happy when I say the words that it's hard to feel any regret.

"Girlfriend!" He responds, reaching out and shaking Thalia's hand. "Wow, you are a lovely lady. What are you doing with this bozo?"

"Hey," I say, narrowing my eyes, but a smile cracks across my lips. Mr. Johnston claps me on the shoulder with a laugh.

"I'm just joking with you, kid. It's great to meet you, Thalia."

"Likewise...I'm sorry, I didn't catch your name." She looks genuinely embarrassed to be admitting so and gives me a glare when I grin.

"Alec didn't tell you? Once a delinquent, always a delinquent. I'm Hal Johnston. I was Alec's music teacher back in the day."

"Music teacher?" Thalia asks, flashing me another glance. I just shrug in response. I'll let her put the rest of the pieces together. "So you went to Malibu High?"

"Wow, do you tell your lovely girlfriend anything Alec?" Mr. Johnston shakes his head, taking a seat behind his desk. "Yep, Alec went here for a few years and spent most of that time in this very room. Such a talented guitar player. You should come back and teach my current students a thing or two, Alec, they could really benefit from a good role model."

He sighs, leaning back in his seat, arms crossed behind his head. "So what brings you back to my class?"

"We're here to ask what you might need from us," I say with a faint smile. "We have a benefit event coming up this Friday, and I've decided that the proceeds are going to go toward this very class. First, I'd like to get more instruments and replace some of the older ones. But eventually I'd also like to redo the room as a whole—better seating, new equipment, innovative technology. So we came to ask you first if you're missing anything specific."

Mr. Johnston looks at me in shock. When I turn to Thalia, she's also looking at me, but there's a curious expression on her face, a cross between questioning and respecting.

"You don't have to do that for us," Mr. Johnston says finally, his voice soft and grateful. "But you know you're like a son to me Alec, and I appreciate everything you've already done. If you really plan on doing this...then thank you. Thank you so much."

I shrug, feeling a little embarrassed, but full of appreciation for the man. "It's the least I can do. For, you know, all the help you provided for me over the years."

Mr. Johnston smiles and nods. "It's no trouble, Alec. You're a good man. We're hoping to finally build a larger guitar program next year, actually. You know we've always had a decent band and orchestra program outlined, but our guitar group is smaller, without enough instruments to go around and match the enthusiasm. But it's in high demand—the kids seem to have so much enthusiasm when they're signing up for classes. I know how much you loved that old thing I lent to you your freshman year."

I couldn't forget it—the guitar had been cracked and beaten up but I had played it almost every night, ignoring my homework in favor of strumming out Radiohead songs in my bedroom.

"It was my favorite," I agreed, giving him a grateful smile. "So you need guitars. That's good to know. I'll let you know how the benefit goes—hopefully we'll raise enough to have the whole class outfitted with an instrument of their own."

Mr. Johnston's eyes gleam. He stands and claps me on the shoulder before giving Thalia a wide smile. "Thank you, Alec."

His appreciation is enough of a boost to make me forget all the darker moments of my past that being in this school brings to light. We leave the building feeling lighter, and full of hope.

# Chapter Six

Thalia

Alec is undeniably cold and closed off. There's something that he doesn't want to talk about, that makes him feel vulnerable and exposed, and I know that it has to do with his past. He's rude and blunt and cruel—all facts that I've come to know in the past week or so that I've spent working with Sound Connections. But while he's not my favorite person to be around, there's something about him that draws me in and holds me close. I can't put my finger on it. Why do I feel so curious about the past he's keeping hidden from me? Why was it so unsurprising to see Mr. Johnston in awe of him, tenderness clear in his gaze?

As we drive away from the school, I keep my hands in my lap and my eyes on the road. Alec is quiet beside me, clearly thinking something through on his end as well. It had been eye opening, seeing that high school and the lack of resources that they so clearly need, when my own childhood had been full of nothing but opportunity. It only makes me feel more excited about the work that we're doing. I want to make a difference, a real difference, and if Alec will let me do it through Sound Connections, then I'm going to take him up on that opportunity.

Sure, he's an asshole at times, but there's a different side to him, one that makes me realize just why Megan stands by him, why his company is doing so well, why Mr. Johnston lit up when he saw Alec. It's clear that he's real and that he wants to change the world for the better.

I glance at Alec from the corner of my eye, trying to gauge what he might be thinking about. He flips through radio stations, face flat and expressionless. He's not driving back to the office. Instead, he turns onto the highway, the bright evening turning into gold around us as the sun begins to set.

"Where are we going?" I ask over the music.

"Dinner, remember? We need to make another public appearance. And apparently, you need to show me how to use a knife and fork, so I don't look like a barbarian in front of the heirs to the Crest toothpaste empire, or whatever."

I can't help it—I laugh. "Crest empire? Where did you get that?"

Alec shrugs. "I mean, even people who invent toothpaste have to listen to music sometimes, don't they?"

I shake my head, laughing still. "You're ridiculous," I say, and I catch a fleeting smile on his face before I glance back at the road, watching the city lights blink around us, seagulls squawking overhead.

"Why did you choose Sound Connections?" He asks, voice somber. "Correct me if I'm wrong, but it seems that you could have had any internship you wanted. I mean, your dad owns half of the rental properties along the coastline. Why not work for him?"

I cross my arms over my chest, as if trying to hold myself together. This question always gets to me. It's intense, resounding. But I don't blame him for asking—Alec and I are different in that way. My family has been well off my whole life. His money is all his, made over the past few years, still fresh.

"I have no interest in politics, real estate, or medicine," I say quickly, keeping my voice even. "My parents' careers are not my own. I know how lucky I am to have grown up the way that I did, but I never asked for those things, and no one ever asked me what I wanted to do. They always assumed for me. They always pushed me in a different direction. I wanted to make a choice that was all mine, and I was drawn to the nonprofit work that Sound Connections supports."

Alec makes a little sound of acknowledgment as he pulls up to the restaurant, a fancy seaside place called Levio. He shifts the car into park.

"That's fair," he says. "Though I still think you're a snob."

I scoff. "Good. I think you're a snob, too."

He presses a hand over his chest and rolls his eyes, pretending to feel wounded. Then he slips from the car, sliding a pair of sunglasses over his eyes. Before I can get out he's walking over to my door and opening it for me. I blink at him, surprised, before he says, "Cameras, dearest."

Right. It's all fake, all a charade, just him posing as the imaginary perfect boyfriend. My mother is going to lose her mind when she sees these photos in the press. But I accept the hand he stretches out toward me and I let him lead me into the restaurant where a hostess is waiting to seat us.

She takes us to a secluded table on the outdoor patio and I watch as her gaze lingers over Alec, clearly liking what she sees. A strange part of me wants to put my hand on his arm, smile at him like he's mine, to show her that she needs to back off. But it's not the truth—what I have with Alec is just a publicity stunt, just a way to make the people fall in love with the product and the cause that we're putting out into the world.

Still—I feel like I'm on fire.

The waitress walks away after taking our drink orders and I cross my legs under the table. Alec's eyes are focused on my cheek. I reach up instinctively to brush my fingers over whatever imperfection he must have spotted there.

"Why do you look so upset?" Alec asks.

"I'm not upset," I answer quickly, realizing that maybe he caught the jealousy on my face. "I'm just—focused. Let's talk about etiquette. Friday's dinner is going to be served, so you need to know how to properly interact with others as you're eating."

I think back to all the dinner parties my parents forced me to join, as the only child who needed to represent all their lifelong efforts. How many conversations, glasses of wine, and louder than life laughs I had to put out into the world.

"Pick up your fork," I say, and Alec surprisingly does as I tell him to, though there's a sour look on his face. He holds the utensil like it's a weapon. I can't stop the grin that spreads across my lips.

"What could you possibly be laughing at?" He grits out between clenched teeth.

"The fork isn't going to bite you," I say. He rolls his eyes. "You need to hold it a little more like…" I try to show him, but the message clearly isn't clicking. Instead, I reach across the table and correct his hand, feeling the heat of his skin against mine, the calloused pad of his thumb. I try not to shiver, but I do, a little, and I glance around as if blaming it on the breeze.

"There, that's better," I say. I feel my cheeks heating as I let go of his hand. He eyes the fork like it's an unfamiliar animal.

"Why are there so many rules? Why can't I just eat like a normal human being?"

"Because people expect more from you," I say, flushing, feeling like my mother as I speak and hating every second of it. "You're an example. They want you to be put together—they want you to show them that you live in luxury and that it has affected you. They want to know that the two of you are the same, that you love the world you live in, that you're prepared to act according to the unspoken rules it provides."

Alec watches me as I speak, his eyes a deep blown-out blue. They're hard to look away from, so I hold his gaze.

"I think it's stupid," he says curtly.

Annoyance rises in me. "Well, so do I, but we don't exactly get a choice, do we?"

"You think it's stupid?" He asks me, like it's a test.

"Of course I do. But just because it's ridiculous doesn't mean I can't understand, or that I can't perform it. It's just an act, Alec. You're just giving people what they want to make sure that they'll trust and respect you. Is that so awful to consider?"

"Yes," he says, low under his breath. "I want them to trust and respect me as I am."

Well so do I! I want to shout. But instead, I shrug. "It's not easy, but it's part of the business. We're selling you and what you stand for. People don't want a faulty product."

He shakes his head as the waitress returns to take our dinner orders.

"How are those drinks?" She asks, a hand trailing close to Alec's shoulder. I almost expect her to reach out and ruffle his hair. "Are you ready to pick out your meal?" She says directly to Alec, as if I'm not even there.

"Yes, I'm ordering for my boyfriend tonight," I say with a smarmy smile. Her eyes flicker over to me with irritation. Alec's eyes follow too, but there's something else in them, unspoken and strange. "I'll have the lobster bisque and the radicchio salad. He'll have the ribeye with roasted vegetables." I hand the menu back to her. "Thank you!"

She walks away with a grimace of a smile. Alec scoffs under his breath. "What if I was a vegetarian?"

I roll my eyes. "You don't get that buff eating only vegetables."

He looks down at his bicep, a teasing eyebrow raised. "What about Popeye? Wasn't he on a spinach diet?"

I laugh, a genuine sound, and he looks caught off guard by my echoing joy. I hide my smile behind my hand. "You're so dumb," I say, still giggling.

He smiles back, and it's the first time I've seen him look anything but cold and contained. "Yeah, I guess I am," he answers.

I could reach across this table right now and take his hand. I could say that it's for the cameras. I could give into the feeling that keeps creeping up my spine, nudging me forward, urging me to touch him. But what would be the point? I don't even like Alec, not like that, even if he is starting to grow on me as a person. But a little voice in the back of my head keeps saying a word that terrifies me: mine.

But to my surprise, Alec beats me to it. He takes my hand in his as the waitress walks back to the table with our food. She takes one look at our intertwined fingers and stalks back to the kitchen, after barely muttering an enjoy over her shoulder in our direction.

"Thank god," Alec says, pulling his hand back to start eating. "I thought she might never stop batting her eyelashes at me."

I laugh around a bite of salad, a hand held in front of my mouth. Alec's eyes narrow. "Why do you keep doing that?" He asks.

I quickly chew and swallow. "Doing what?"

"Covering your mouth when you laugh or smile."

I feel my ears go hot, though I don't know what I have to be embarrassed about. "I don't know, I guess I just—it's rude for me to not cover it up. I'm eating, I don't want you to see something in my mouth, you know?"

He shakes his head. "Seems like a waste. You're hiding a pretty smile."

Now I'm really turning crimson. I shrug, not trusting myself to speak out loud. "I don't know, it's just how I was raised."

He makes a noise under his breath, some grunt of disagreement, and takes a big bite of his steak.

"You should try to take small, measured bites," I say, wanting to regain control of the situation. "It makes it easier to take breaks in between to make conversation."

"I don't want to converse with anyone," he says around a mouthful of steak. I cringe.

"Well, you're going to have to if you want to sway them to donate."

He shrugs. "If you say so."

I sigh. "Megan is going to have my head if you don't act right at this dinner."

"Listen, I'll be on my best behavior, okay? I don't want the benefit to fail, either. I'm remembering the things you say. I'll incorporate them during the dinner. Got it?"

"Sure," I say, still feeling unsure, still wanting him to prove me wrong. We eat in the quiet for a while, enjoying the distant sound of waves, the beach never far. Some of the people in Malibu might be terrible, but this is my home, and every night is something beautiful.

He pays at the end of dinner and helps me up from my seat as we head back to the car. I catch sight of paparazzi toward the entrance of the restaurant. I wonder if Megan hired them again for publicity, or if they're starting to catch on to who Alec is.

He keeps his hand on the small of my back as we walk, an action that sends a little thrill up my spine. I hold my head high and lean into him as we walk, listening as camera shutters click in our wake. The moon is high and bright overhead. The night is clear and beautiful, the breeze chilly but soothing, the heat of Alec beside me enough to make me want to wrap my arms around him.

But instead, Alec stops me by his car. He turns to me and touches my chin with a gentle finger. I blink up at him, surprised, but I barely have time to inhale before he leans into me.

He pauses right before his lips meet mine. "Can I kiss you?" He asks, his breath ghosting over my lips. My stomach does a somersault. I don't know what to do, don't know what to say, so I just let the word burst from my lips.

"Yes," I say.

His kiss is softer than I thought it would be. But as his lips meet mine I feel the zing of him all the way through my body, the electric heat of him on me. The hand on my waist pulls me closer while the one on my chin holds me in place. It's only a matter of seconds but I'm on fire, every inch of me wanting to fold into him.

"There," he says as he pulls away, and that's when I notice the flash of the camera going off in every direction. "Now they have their million-dollar photo."

"Yeah," I say, laughing breathlessly. But my heart is louder than a lightning strike in my chest.

# Chapter Seven

Alec

I don't know what possessed me to kiss Thalia. There was just something about that dinner, about that moment, that made me feel immortal and powerful. Something about looking into her eyes and seeing that vivid smile. I don't know when I stopped hating her, when I started to tolerate her presence. But now, I don't know how to go back in time and make things the way they used to be.

It's all for show. I know that, she knows that. The public might not know, but what they don't realize won't hurt them. As long as we're on the same page, we'll be fine, right?

The drive home is charged with a strange energy. Thalia gives me her address and I start to wind through downtown Malibu, past the small houses and neighborhoods where I grew up toward the more spread-out villas that she's used to. Thalia sits beside me, her eyes trained on the world flitting by past the rolled down window, breeze ruffling her hair. It gives me a chance to flick my eyes over in her direction every once in a while. I study her profile from the corner of my gaze when we stop at a red light. There's a faint smile ghosting across her lips, and I remember the heat that unfurled in my chest when I pressed that kiss to her lips. I can't explain it—why I did it, why it affected me so greatly. All I know is that when I turned to her in front of all those cameras, there was an impulsive desire burning strong inside of me. I had to kiss her. I had to show all those leeches aching to get a photo of us that she was mine, and that it was the two of us as a pair and that was it.

I shake my head slowly, trying to knock the thought like cobwebs from my mind. It's a foolish idea, one that I need to stop considering. We're not together and we never will be. It's all a front, a publicity stunt to make the company grow.

"Something wrong?" Thalia asks as she turns to face me. I wish I knew her better, that I could read her face and understand what she's thinking. This woman is supposed to be my "girlfriend" and I can barely even tell if she stills thinks I'm an untouchable asshole.

And why wouldn't she? What reason have I given her to believe otherwise? It's better this way, to keep her at a distance and keep myself safe. I don't need anyone in my business, especially not a rich socialite who's used to getting everything that she wants.

"Nothing's wrong," I answer, a beat too late. "I'm fine."

Thalia laughs a little, like she doesn't believe me. But she doesn't push the subject and I'm thankful for that. At least she's gotten to know me well enough by now to know that when I say I'm fine, I don't want to hear anything else about it.

Even though it's dark by now, I can tell how lavish the houses are around here. What isn't wide and expansive is obscured by old trees given the luxury of space to grow. The stars overhead are bright and blinking back at us, guiding the way.

Truth be told, I don't live too far from here now. My new apartment is nothing like these sprawling mansions, but it's leagues nicer than the place where I was raised. It's spacious and refined and it's everything that I thought I would never have. But despite all the money that Sound Connections has earned me, I'd rather give it back—I can just put it into our benefit, instead of some huge and empty house that I'd rarely be at.

When we finally pull up to the address that Thalia gave me, it's an enormous house, villa-style. The entire property is gated off, and warm lights line a drive and a path that leads up to the door.

"Right here is fine," Thalia says, avoiding my eyes and sliding her seat belt off. "Thanks for dinner and the ride. I'll see you tomorrow?"

"Tomorrow," I agree. Then, against my better judgement, I find myself saying: "I had a good time. Enjoy the rest of your night, Thalia."

She steps out of the car and gives me a look that I almost can't decipher. Her dark eyes are heavy and knowing, like she can feel the unspoken words that are caught in my mouth, the kiss that we shared still tingling between us. Things have changed—that much is obvious. But it feels like speaking it aloud would give the idea too much power, and neither of us are willing to do that.

"Thank you, Alec," she says finally. A gentle smile slips onto her lips. "Have a good night."

Then she shuts the car door behind her and punches in a code at the gate. I watch as she makes her way up the winding path until she disappears inside of the ornate front door.

It takes a moment for me to gather my thoughts and pull away from her house, but I finally do, heading back the same direction I came until I'm finally at my own apartment.

I fall into bed soon after arriving, feeling exhausted. But sleep won't come—my mind keeps replaying the sensation of our kiss until finally I'm too tired to keep running on a loop.

The next morning, I blearily blink myself awake. The sun streams through my blinds and fills the apartment with stark warm light. I shower and get dressed, shaving my jaw in the mirror, fixing my hair with a touch of gel. I arrive at the office early and spend the first hour researching which guitars would be best for the class so that we're ready to place an order as soon as the benefit is wrapped up. I'll be making a sizeable donation myself, but it's still not enough to give each kid a guitar that they can carry between home and class, along with enough for traveling performances.

"Morning, boss," Megan says happily from my doorway. She raps on the door with a firm hand. "Can I come in?"

"Looks like you're already halfway in here," I say, but there's no venom behind it. Megan slips in easily, her pants swishing together as she walks. She takes the seat across from my desk.

"It's time to go public," she says, definitively.

"Huh?"

"With the relationship. You need to make a public statement."

"What were all the paparazzi photos if not a public statement?" I ask, an eyebrow raised. "Was that just us playing pretend?"

Megan sighs. Clearly I've disappointed her in some media sphere.

"The public knows that you and Thalia are rumored to be together. But that's all it is—it's a rumor meant to stir up interest, to get people speculating and talking. And now we need to confirm the relationship. Thalia is a high profile person in this city, with her father running for mayor, and it will look good to show that you're connected to high society. We'll have journalists and big names showing up tomorrow night, needing to know the scoop."

It makes sense, from Megan's backwards point of view. Still, I sigh.

"So what am I supposed to do about that? Send out a press release?"

Megan shakes her head. "No, nothing that complicated. You just need to make an Instagram post and tag Thalia in it."

I grimace. That's honestly almost worse.

"Fine. But what are we going to post? Some watermarked paparazzi photo?"

Megan shakes her head again, a sly smile on her face. "Nope. We're having a photoshoot today. You and Thalia will be visiting the Malibu Botanical Garden and a photographer with take some pictures that we'll release tonight. That way, everyone will be scrambling to attend tomorrow's event and see the mysterious girl on your arm."

I roll my eyes, but Megan cuts me off before I can speak. "Have I ever led you astray, Alec? Trust me on this. It's a smart strategy, even if you don't see it yet. But all our hard work will be worth it in the end when we're building a new music wing over at Malibu High."

She gets up and makes her way over to the door. "As usual, Thalia will be here at noon—be ready to leave with her."

There's no use fighting Megan when she's like this, if the past week has proven anything to me. So I keep working until it's time to go. Thalia meets me by the front door of the building, looking fresh and light in a long floral dress. Her hair falls in ringlets around her face. Part of me wants to reach out and tuck a strand behind her ear, but instead I stick my hand in my pockets.

"I assume Megan filled you in," I say by way of greeting and Thalia nods.

"It's time to play the part," Thalia says with a laugh.

I lead her over to the car. By now, it's starting to feel natural, driving around with her and watching Malibu pass by around us. It's like I'm re-mapping the place where I grew up, learning the landscape all over again. It's a surreal feeling, but one that is starting to feel right.

"I've never been to this garden, but I hear that it's beautiful," Thalia says wistfully as we pull up. I grimace.

"Yeah, sure it might be beautiful, but it's probably full of bugs," I answer with a barely repressed shudder.

"Oh my god, are you scared of bugs?"

"Of course not," I snap back quickly.

"That's rich. You're literally like, six two and completely tatted up and you can't handle a bee or a fly?"

"You're making assumptions that are likely to get you fired," I shoot back at her, but her grin doesn't falter. She looks delighted to have this information, no matter how many times I deny it.

We meet the photographer by a lily pad-laden pond at the center of the park. The sun is high and hot overhead and dragonflies move lazily across the water. I eye them suspiciously as Thalia nearly skips ahead, her head tipped back to drink in the afternoon light.

"Ahh, it's so beautiful here. I've been in a stuffy classroom all morning and I needed some time outside."

I raise my eyebrows in her direction as the photographer waves us over. "I didn't realize you had class before this."

"And after, too, some evenings," Thalia answers, gazing out over the water. "It's not so bad. I'm almost finished with my degree."

We shake hands with the photographer and he sets us up at a small archway, where flowers grow across lattice in beautiful winding patterns.

"I never went to college," I admit against Thalia's ear as he sets us up in an embrace that's supposed to be candid but feels anything but. I can feel her heart beating against my chest. "What's it like?"

"Smile," the photographer says, and I try to do so without looking like I'm baring my teeth.

"It's fun," Thalia says, her voice a soft hum beneath my chin. "Though, I suppose I haven't exactly had the most typical college experience. I lived on campus the first two years, but then my dad pulled me out of the dorm and made me move back home. He was afraid I'd get caught at some party drinking underage or smoking weed, and that I'd ruin his whole reputation and election cycle."

I'm surprised by that—Thalia seems like anything but a party girl. In fact, she often seems too uptight.

"I guess it's a good thing I didn't go," I say. "All I did was drink and smoke growing up, even throughout high school. Your dad would have hated me."

She laughs. The sound is sweet as a windchime. "You're not wrong, I guess. Though I think you would have thrived in college. Every girl would have been head over heels for you."

I shrug, but the photographer scolds me, repositioning us in a different embrace. Thalia looks like a natural in every pose he sets up for us. I, on the other hand, feel entirely out of my element, and I'm sure it shows on my face.

"I doubt that," I answer once we're finally in position. Thalia's hand is on my shoulder, and I can feel the heat that travels through the tips of her fingers down my spine. "I know what I look like. I'm terrifying."

She laughs again, and I try to ignore the satisfaction that rises in my chest every time I know that laugh is because of me.

"Yeah, totally terrifying," she scoffs, voice close to my ear. The photographer steps close to us and arranges Thalia's hands—her palm presses against my hip, her knee brushing mine. She tips back her head until the light hits her cheek and smiles wide. She looks radiant, a fact that I have to ignore in order to keep myself held together.

"These are great," the photographer says with a satisfied nod. "Megan will love them. You two are done for the day."

Thalia pulls back immediately, tucking her hands in the pockets of her long floral dress. She looks a little sheepish, like she was embarrassed to be so intimately close to me. I step back, giving her space—I'm not going to make her uncomfortable if she doesn't want to be around me.

It's all pretend, I have to think, the words playing on a loop in my head. None of this is real.

But there's a traitorous stutter to my heart. I'm starting to think that maybe I don't hate Thalia after all—and that's a dangerous thought to have.

# Chapter Eight

Thalia

The photos of Alec and I are released that same night. Even I have to admit that we look like two people madly in love—my hands on him look natural, and he's even smiling in some of the pictures, a genuine thing that catches me off guard every time I spot it.

Megan posted the photos on Instagram and they racked up thousands of likes and comments in minutes. Though I try to hold back, afraid of what they might say, my hands move against my will and scroll through the words left behind by random people all over the internet. As I lay in my bed that night, music playing somewhere distantly in the house I share with my parents, I read each one.

OMG, they're so cute! One comment reads, and I can't help the satisfied smile that cracks across my face. I believe in love again, another reads. I want someone to look at me like Alec is looking at her.

I almost can't believe that our photos are working, that they're convincing people we're a real couple. But then I look through them again. We seem so comfortable together for two people who hated each other barely more than a week ago. We look good, standing side by side like that, his tattoos dark and prominent against his skin where his arm wraps around me and the sun lighting me up in a hundred different shades of gold. My dress fits me like a glove. Alec's pants are pressed and neat, and his hair falls into an easy coif. We look like a real couple. And, shockingly, I find myself suddenly wanting all of it again—his arms around me, the easy way we made each other laugh.

It's been so long since I was in a real relationship, and even the ones I had in the past were nothing impressive. Every man I've been with always made me feel like an accessory, something disposable and annoying. But even with the rocky start I had with Alec, I feel more comfortable around him in a matter of days than I did spending months dating other men.

But it's a fake relationship, engineered to create buzz, nothing more. There's no use getting sucked into something that was never real to begin with and never would be. Right?

I turn over in bed, lying on my side and flipping through the photos of us. I want to be as happy as the Thalia in those photos. And even though my brain tells me it's a stupid thought, I suddenly want to kiss Alec again. His lips had felt so right on mine, his eyes dark and piercing, his hand firm and comforting. A kiss for the cameras is just acting. But somehow, it had still felt real.

As I swipe down, I notice a few comments that go in a different direction.

This whole thing looks posed, one reads. They're so awkward together.

I cringe reading it and close my phone, feeling even more confused than I had that afternoon while we were taking the photos. Why can't it just be simple? Why couldn't Alec have been a normal boss, that I could just keep hating up until the moment I had the pleasure of quitting?

It doesn't matter, regardless. This is a job. A job I signed up for to forward my career and to help others, not to find some forbidden romance in the midst of my work. The event is tomorrow, and what truly matters is Alec raising money for the charity, not my weirdly developing feelings for him.

I press my cheek into the pillow and let my eyes flutter shut. I need to sleep. Tomorrow has to be perfect, so that I can show everyone exactly why I deserve this job.

But before I can drift off to sleep, a knock sounds at the door. My mother pushes her way in before I can answer, and I sit up, blinking at the hall light that floods in as she enters.

"Hi honey," she says briskly, coming over to perch on the end of my bed. "Can you tell me why I'm seeing photos of you with this man you're working with online? Dad's assistant showed me—you two are in a relationship?"

I swallow hard around the lump in my throat—if I tell her the truth, I'll only get a lecture about how Alec is taking advantage of me and my place in the company. How this kind of thing could destroy my future and my opportunities in politics. Opportunities that I've never even wanted in the first place. Even if I told her that it was Megan's plan for us, I already know that she'd never believe me.

"Yes," I say, instead of trying to explain. "We're dating. He's a great man."

"Honey...you've known him for what, a week? You're going to end up getting hurt. And he's very...different."

I roll my eyes. "Mother, he's no different than you or I. He's a great man. And we're just getting to know each other and spending time together—that's what dating is all about, isn't it?"

She squints her eyes at me, suspicious. "If you say so, darling. Please be careful. I'll have Dad's attorney do a background check on this Alec man—you need to ensure your safety."

"Mother, that's not necessary," I answer quickly. But she's already standing with her hand reaching for the doorknob.

"I'm just looking out for you, dear. Maybe you should invite Alec over for dinner soon so we can get to know him in person, too. Get some rest now."

She closes the door behind her with a firm click and I blink back at her in surprise, feeling ambushed. I don't know much about Alec's past, but I have a feeling that they're not going to like what they see there.

That night I sleep restlessly, my eyes shut but my mind still running a mile a minute. When I wake I feel like I barely slept at all. But there's a whole day to go through before tonight's event, and my heart is already pounding by the time I'm out the door with coffee and a bagel, rushing to my car to make it to class before nine.

Class passes by quickly, though I catch a few stares in my direction when I first walk into the lecture. Sound Connections is a huge app when it comes to users my age, so I'm not surprised that a few of them might follow Alec and keep up with the content that he shares. I guess they just never expected that content to be one of their classmates.

My professor, however, is oblivious, so we spend the whole class studying patterns in media while I get to shrink into the background. I take vigorous notes but my mind won't stop wandering to the coming evening. I'll have to go by the office and change into whatever outfit Megan has planned for me. Alec will put on the tux that we picked together. And we'll all attend the event and wow the crowd until Alec's name is the number one winner of the night.

He'll wow them. I know it. And if he doesn't...I might be out of a job.

I pack up after class and hurry over to the office. Once inside, I feel the chaos wash over me. Everyone is in rush mode—people dart back and forth, tied to their phones as they attempt to confirm with caterers and chair delivery and banner sizes. Megan is talking animatedly to someone through a Bluetooth headset, her hands waving in front of her as she speaks. I weave my way through the halls and past the conference room until I'm finally at Alec's office. I knock once and let myself in when he answers.

"Hello," he says, his eyes flicking to me when I step inside and close the door behind me. He looks nice, hair already done and his jaw clean shaven, but there are slight bags under his eyes. I wonder if he spent the whole night just as sleepless as I was.

"You look tired," I say, the first thing that springs to mind.

"Gee, thanks," he answers with a scoff. "You look great yourself."

"Sorry. It's just—you know, it's my job to notice things like these. Do you need a coffee? Lunch?"

"What I need is a full body massage," Alec says with a groan as he rubs a hand over the back of his neck. Then, as it seems to register what he's just said to me, he adds, "I mean, not from you. Just in general."

I raise an eyebrow, unable to resist teasing him. "What, are you saying I don't give good massages?"

His cheeks tinge with color. I feel a flush of pride rise in me, that I was able to affect him with my words alone. Then I shove the feeling down just as quickly.

"Let's just forget I ever said that," he responds gruffly. "Is everything set for tonight?"

I nod, straightening my back, like we're entering "professional" mode. "It seems that we're good to go. Fender has agreed to work with us in the event that we raise enough money to purchase all the guitars for the school. They've also agreed to help us start setting up a fund for replacing the rest of the instruments and expanding Malibu High's collection."

Alec nods, satisfied. "Good. I'm glad to hear it. And you?"

"Me?" I ask, blinking back at him.

"How are you feeling? I know you didn't exactly sign up to be my, um, pretend girlfriend. I just wanted to make sure you feel comfortable with tonight."

I keep blinking back at him, unsure of what to say. "Oh, yes, I'm fine. It's fine. Everything's—"

"Fine?" He finishes, smiling. "That's good to hear, but I don't want your work here to be fine, Thalia. I want you to enjoy it. I know we have our—differences, but that doesn't mean you shouldn't have a job that you believe in. I just wanted to make sure that you're happy."

I feel stunned. Happy? Well, yes, I suppose I am. Looking at him, regal and smiling behind his desk, makes me know that for sure. I'm happy, and I love my job despite the short amount of time I've been doing it. I don't want to mess this up.

"Of course I'm happy," I say, and then because the moment feels too vulnerable I have to change the subject. "Speaking of tonight, we need to do a check in: tux?"

"Got it," Alec says solemnly.

"Friendly smile? Manners? A general lack of iciness?"

"What is this, a popularity contest?" He replies with a grimace.

"Well, yes, kind of," I say, smiling. "Except you're going to be the most popular boy in school and everyone will be vying to be your friend."

"Great," Alec says, his voice dead and faint, "there's a first time for everything."

I roll my eyes, though it's impossible to hide the smile that curls at the corners of my lips. He waves a dismissive hand at me. "Okay, go, get out of here and get ready. I won't forget everything you taught me in the next four hours. I'll see you later."

I nod and do as he says—he is still my boss, no matter which way I try to look at it. I return to Megan's office to find a dress laid out with my name on it—Thalia, in big blue sharpie on a little green note. It's beautiful. The fabric is gauzy and pale and embroidered with subtle stars. It's a dress fit for a queen, and I feel like anything but. Yet I still gather it in my arms, holding it close to my chest and smiling down at the fabric.

I spend the next few hours getting prepared. I run errands for others around the office, dropping off mail and picking up coffee and talking a few people down when the pressure starts to build. Then, as we get closer to event time, Megan lets me use her office to change. I slip into the dress and marvel at myself in the mirror that hangs on her wall—I look like I belong here, with them. I look like anyone but my parents' daughter. And for the first time in a long time, I am happy.

Cars pick us up and take us to the event as the sun starts to set. The benefit is being held in a grand banquet hall downtown and the whole place is decked out in beautiful florals and bright candles, with banners bearing the Sound Connections logo and color palette. Everything is tinted in the periwinkle blue of our branding, and it makes the room feel like it's underwater, or like a pale dawn sky is rising around us. It's beautiful.

"They did a great job," Alec says as he comes up behind me. He places a hand on the small of my back—he looks stunning, like a model stepping straight off a magazine cover. The blue suit really does wonders for his complexion. I suddenly want to run my fingers through his dark hair, muss it up, feel the heat of his skin beneath mine. But instead I just nod and smile.

"It's stunning," I say, meaning it. He grins.

"Think it's pretty enough to woo some rich people to give me their money?"

"Oh yes," I say with a sly smile. "They won't be able to stop throwing bills your way."

"Let's put your theory to the test," he says, and he leads me further into the room.

# Chapter Nine

Alec

I almost expected everyone to be fashionably late to the benefit dinner—but against my expectations, people begin showing up right at the eight p.m. start time.

Thalia looks incredible in the dress that Megan picked out, and I find myself proud that I get to walk around with her on my arm. I didn't expect myself to be so thrilled by the prospect of pretending to be hers all night, but now I'm grateful for it. With Thalia beside me, I don't have to face any of these snobs alone, and I just might be able to keep my cool long enough to raise some real money.

I catch sight of Megan greeting people and ushering them in. There are names set out at round dining tables and huge bouquets standing in the center of them. Waiters drift by us with trays of champagne and I snatch two flutes, handing one to Thalia and knocking the other back in a quick flutter of movements.

"Liquid courage?" Thalia teases, as she sips her own. I grimace and nod.

"We'll need it. You'll see, very soon."

As if on cue, the last person that I wanted to see tonight comes up to us, walking like he owns the place. I can admit it—he looks sleek in a black tux, his hair gelled back in pale blond waves, a permanent smirk etched onto his mouth.

"Alec Lynch," he says. "Good to see you, my man."

I reach for Thalia, my fingers curling into her side, and I'm pleased when she rewards me by playing her part and leaning into me with a warm smile. "Who's this, honey? I don't think we've had the pleasure of meeting."

"Matthew Torres, but you can call me Matt, beautiful. I've been a contemporary of your...boyfriend's for longer than you've been out of high school, it seems."

He smiles when he says it, the same smug Torres that I've known for years. I watch Thalia's eyes narrow though her own soft smile stays on her face. Her gaze is powerful—inquisitive, calculating, understanding.

"You two must have known each other for a long time, then," Thalia challenges. "I'm surprised I've never heard your name before now."

It's Torres's turn to show his annoyance. He pushes his hands deeper into his pants pockets. "You might not know my name, but surely you know my platform—I created Songbird."

Songbird is a rival company of Sound Connections—they advertise the same connections through music taste, but they don't have the same nuanced dynamics that we've created through our playlist platform and the way it connects potential lovers together. Torres thinks that we're the same, but truly he just can't see his own faults.

"Doesn't ring a bell," Thalia says sweetly, and I want to kiss her right then and there in front of the entire room, to show my appreciation for her pulling through.

Torres looks affronted. His eyes narrow, just slightly. "So how long have you two been together? You must have met recently, or I would have seen you at Alec's last event. Though, maybe you stayed home then, to avoid the fool Alec made himself out to be when he got into an argument with one of the richest men in the city." He laughs, like he's making a joke, but I know that it's all just a well-aimed barb. He's referring to his father, Harold Torres, the man who funded his son's entire venture without blinking an eye. The last time I saw him, he made a comment about me looking like a hoodlum. It's not my fault that I told him his mistress made him look like a crypt keeper in comparison.

"You're right," Thalia says, looking up at me with bright eyes. "We haven't been together long. But every moment that we've spent together has been an absolute dream. Alec is the kindest man I know, with the biggest heart. I'm so excited to be supporting his charity this evening with all of your generous donations."

Torres's head tips back slightly, caught off guard. "I'm very glad to hear it," he answers slowly, like he's thinking through his next words. "And Songbird is happy to leave a donation by the end of the night. I'm excited to see what you both will do with the money."

I smile, and it's a plastered-on thing but at least it's there. While I'm thankful for Thalia speaking up, I can't let her do all the talking. "We're thankful that you came this evening," I say, my voice deep and cold despite the warm words. "Please enjoy the food and have a wonderful time."

Torres nearly sneers at me. But he nods at the last second, schooling his expression. "Thank you. I will. I hope you two lovebirds have a great rest of your night."

I pull Thalia in closer to my side, a reflex that seems to surprise both of us. She looks up at me again with a wide smile. Torres's eyes drag over us, and I suddenly feel like he's looking right through me and seeing everything that I'm attempting to hide. But I can't let him get to me. I have to do what Thalia taught me—show up, impress the people I hate most, and snatch their money out from under their noses to help the ones who really need it.

"You did good," Thalia murmurs, as Torres walks away. "Though, he seems like a slimy man."

I chuckle. "Yeah, you could say that. He's been trying to convince his father to buy out my company for years so his shittier version of it can dominate the market. But we're doing too well for him to afford it."

Thalia squeezes my bicep, a sly look in her eyes. "Good. That's what I like to hear."

"Thalia! Alec! Let's get a picture!" Megan calls suddenly, materializing with a photographer at the center of the room. The photographer leans in and snaps a photo of us, the flash nearly blinding me. Thalia's hand is on my arm, mine around her waist, and our surprised smiles are bright and honest.

Megan smiles at me in return. She leans close as the photographer moves on and says, "Cute, Lynch. You two look good together. Really good."

I roll my eyes. "Give it up, Reinhardt."

Megan shrugs but her eyes are devious as she waves and leaves us to fend for ourselves.

We mill around the room all night. People recognize Thalia from her parents, and she gets roped into many conversations about the run for mayor and her mother's medical practice. I have to give it to her—I could never hold myself together with all these people hounding me about my family. At least when people are rude to my face, it's because they're reacting to me, not my family's reputation.

I speak with digital investors, stockholders, local musicians and low-level celebrities. We discuss the field, and the charity, and the work that we're doing to try to make a difference. Some of them give me a little hope—that maybe they'll be willing to help even if it doesn't end up benefitting them or building their profits. Others make my skin crawl with their sleazy comments. But with Thalia beside me, I stay on my best behavior. I have civil conversations and I even smile once in a while, trying to convince these elite snobs to split up their fortune and make some lives better. It's worth a try, isn't it?

Against all odds, it seems like the night is going in a positive direction. I feel buoyed by Thalia's stability, her smart comments, and her quick mind. As the event starts to wind down, Megan calls us to the front of the room, where she gently taps a delicate glass with a fork. Then she gestures to me, her smile wide and bright. I raise my eyebrows in question and she gestures again, big sweeping movements with her arms.

"Speech," she hisses through her teeth, smile never faltering. "Talk to them, dummy."

I clear my throat as Megan hands me a microphone. I look out at the room. Everyone is either seated at a table, enjoying their meal, or milling around the hall with a glass in their hands. They're all looking back at me and I feel the weight of their gazes, as heavy as stones on my back.

Then Thalia touches my wrist, and the sensation of her close to me is enough to steady my instinct to lash out against the judging and waiting stares.

"Thank you all for coming tonight," I say into the microphone. My voice is surprisingly steady. I even manage not to grimace as I speak. "I'm so glad that you all came out this evening to support the funding of underprivileged music programs. Everyone at Sound Connections is so grateful for your generosity, and we can't wait to provide the students at Malibu High School with the instruments they've been needing to learn and perform with."

I turn to glance at Thalia, who's smiling at me with an even and encouraging gaze. I want to tip her chin towards me and ask the question that's been plaguing me all day—is she really pretending? Or have things started to change for her like they're changing for me?

"Sound Connections is all about building relationships through interconnectivity," I say, my voice pitched low. "We want to build bridges that will go on to do great things. That's why I'm so grateful to have my beautiful girlfriend by my side—she's the proof that connections really are out there for everyone, even someone like me."

The crowd begins to clap and cheer, a reaction that stuns me. Thalia grins back at me. I catch Megan's eye at the edge of the crowd. She's making a new gesture, one that I recognize as—oh. She wants us to kiss.

Fuck it.

I cup Thalia's cheek with my hand and pull her into me, kissing her hard, putting all the warmth and joy that that moment provides into the touch, feeling her open up beneath me. It's gentle and hot all at once, but I pull away before I can question why I want to go further, slide a hand up her thigh and under her dress, feel her gasp against me.

It's too much. It's not enough. It's a confusing mess.

When I look at her again, I can barely think over the applause and chatter erupting around us. And she's looking at me like—like—like maybe she's thinking exactly what I'm thinking. That the kiss we just shared sent sparks across my skin and heat pooling in my gut. She smiles, her eyes half-lidded, and I wonder how I could have ever despised this girl when all she's ever tried to do was support me.

"Nice one, Alec," she says softly, and I can't help but grin back at her.

The rest of the night passes in a blur. We raise nearly $100,000 from our donors, enough to purchase new guitars for every student and an entire revamp of the instruments they already have. Hell, maybe we'll even get them a bus, so they can travel to different music competitions.

As the crew starts to clean up, Megan finds me downing a final glass of wine, my head just slightly buzzed from the alcohol. She claps me on the back with a hearty laugh.

"You crushed it out there, Lynch. $96,000! Who would have ever thought we'd do that well? You must have really charmed the crowd." She winks at me when she says it, and I'm happy enough that I laugh in response.

"This is just the beginning," I promise her. "Next fundraiser, we'll raise enough to build the entire new music wing. These kids will have the space they deserve."

Megan squeezes my arm. "You're a good man, Alec. I appreciate you going along with my foolish ideas. Didn't I tell you it would work out in the end, and that Thalia would be a huge help?"

"You did," I answer, grinning. I glance around the emptying room. "Speaking of which, where's Thalia?"

"I think I saw her heading outside. You might still be able to catch her."

I thank Megan and hurry outside of the banquet hall. The path that leads to the parking lot is dotted with small solar lights. I spot a figure walking toward the cars beside someone else, her dress glinting under the pale light of the moon. The other person turns and leaves before I can reach them, their shape disappearing into the night.

"Thalia!" I call before I can stop myself. She turns, surprised, and I watch her face light up just a fraction when she spots me.

"Alec," she calls back, her voice warm. I jog over to her.

"Where are you going? Who were you talking to?"

"Oh, I was just going to call a cab," she answers quickly. "And that was Matthew Torres—he wanted to tell me that he thought you and I were good for one another." She makes a face of distaste. "Whatever that means."

The thought of her and Torres speaking alone makes something flare inside of me—jealousy? Rage? What would I have to be jealous about?

"You should stay away from him, he's no good," I say roughly, keeping my eyes trained on her even expression.

"Noted. He doesn't exactly seem like the nicest guy in town," she says with a slight laugh. "What are you doing out here, anyway? I thought you were busy in there."

"No way," I answer with a laugh. "I was dying to leave. Let me give you a ride home."

She blinks in surprise. "You don't have to do that, it's really fine—"

"I want to," I interrupt. "Let me be nice for once."

She rolls her eyes, smiling. "Fine. Just this one time."

I lead her to my car, trying not to feel like my heart is thundering in my ears. Why do I feel so overwhelmed with her near, like she can sense every thump of my pulse, hear my every nervous breath?

We get in the car and I pull away from the event, loosening my bowtie with one hand while I steer with the other. We sit in peaceful quiet, the crickets singing beyond the rolled down windows.

"I know I've been an asshole," I say, because I need to say it, I need to be honest. I hate feeling like I'm living in this lie. "I'm sorry."

Thalia turns to me. I can feel her gaze on my cheek. "It's okay, Alec. You know I don't care. I'm just here to help."

I can think of a hundred other ways she could help me right now, starting with her hands on my belt.

No, no, no. It's not like that. I need to banish that thought from my head.

"Still, I was rude and you were only doing your job. This night couldn't have happened without you there. You made it all possible."

I hear her laugh, softly. "That's sweet of you to say."

"I mean it. We need you at the company. You've managed to revamp our reputation in barely two weeks. I—I need you on my team."

She hums softly. "I'm happy to be on your team, Alec. This job is everything I've ever wanted. And I like...spending time with you. You're good company, you know that?"

My knuckles hurt from gripping the steering wheel. As we drive, I spot the beach coming up, and I make an instinctive move and pull over in the parking lot that faces the water.

"What's wrong?" Thalia asks as we park. Her eyes are worried.

"Can I ask you something?" I say, feeling breathless.

"Of course."

"Do you like kissing me?"

She blinks back at me, her dark eyes so wide and wondering. Her lips part.

"Yes," she says finally, her voice quiet. "Do you like kissing me?"

"Yes," I answer, my voice nearly a growl. "Can I kiss you right now?"

She barely has time to smile and speak her soft please before I'm reaching for her, a hand against her jaw, my mouth on hers. This is different from all the kisses before. I feel like I'm on fire. Her hand curls in my hair and she gasps in my mouth and one of my hands trails along her thigh, the fabric of her dress silky and soft. We kiss for what feels like hours, until I feel like my breath begins and ends with her.

"I don't want to go home," Thalia says when we finally part, and her eyes are nearly glowing in the dark. "I want to go with you."

She doesn't have to tell me twice.

# Chapter Ten

Thalia

The moment Alec spoke his feelings aloud, I felt a weight disappear from my chest, replaced by a humming thrill. His mouth is addictive on mine—I can't stop touching him, can't stop wanting to kiss him, even as he nearly speeds to take us back to his apartment.

His home is just like him—understated and unique. It's a gorgeous apartment, clearly expensive in some ways but still lived in, still real and alive. He unlocks the door in one fluid motion and leads me inside. As soon as the door is closed, the lights still low, he leans into me, his breath ghosting against my cheek.

"Is this okay?" He asks, his voice rough with desire.

"Yes," I whisper, curling my arms around his neck and pulling his mouth down to meet mine.

Every kiss feels like the first—thrilling, dangerous, electric. But this time, these kisses aren't pretend. They're as real as Alec is beneath my hands. His skin is so hot where we touch. I run my hands down his arms, over the inked lines of art that make him who he is, across the defined planes of his back. His stubble brushes my cheek as he leans in to press kisses against my jaw and down my throat. I arch under his touch, wanting more, never able to get enough.

"We shouldn't be doing this," he says quietly, against my ear. "You're my employee."

"We're far past the moral repercussions of whatever we have going on," I say with a low laugh, running a hand down the front of his chest. "Who cares if it's messy? It was always going to be that way, from the first moment we met."

He smiles. In the dark, it's a hungry sight. Suddenly I want him even closer—I want that mouth all over me.

"Can I take you to my bedroom?" He asks against my ear, his voice almost a growl.

"Yes," I gasp, the thrill of his question curling deep in my belly. When he scoops me into his arms, I let out a surprised laugh, hooking an arm around his neck to hold on tight. He carries me down the hall to a dimly lit room, dominated by a king size bed in the center.

I feel like this is the first time we're really looking at each other, without boundaries or nerves or awkwardness. I lay back on Alec's bed as he leans over me and our eyes meet. His gaze is the deep blue of dusk, his mouth red from our kiss, his hair mussed and nearly long enough now to fall into his eyes, my fingers having ruined its style for the evening. His bowtie hangs loose around his neck. He looks commanding, in control, and devastatingly handsome.

"You're beautiful," he says down to me, and it's almost enough to make me laugh. I want to tell him that I was thinking the exact same thing about him. But then he runs his fingers up my bare thigh, bunching up the fabric of my dress, and it takes everything in me not to keen up against him.

"Look at the faces you're making," he says, his voice taking on a new, rougher tone. Suddenly the Alec I thought I knew is gone, replaced by this man with the blown out pupils and warm breath against my lips. "I've barely even touched you yet."

My eyelashes flutter as his thumb grazes the edge of my underwear, where my thigh meets my hip. But just as soon as it appeared his hand is gone and he's kissing me again, hungry and intense. I lose myself in it. I let everything about him wash over me—his spicy scent, the cool silky feeling of his hair against my fingers, the rough graze of his stubble on my jaw.

I sigh under his touch. Everything feels like too much, his lips on mine, his hands firm on my waist. I reach up and tug on his bowtie.

"Take this off," I say, breaking our kiss, and he grins down at me, the expression softening his whole face.

"Say please," he murmurs, covering my hand with his own.

"How about I say now?" I answer, a sly smile on my lips.

"You're demanding even in bed, huh?"

Though he pretends to be annoyed, I know his expressions well enough by now to tell when he's really angry. And this is all for show, because he leans away from me with a finger slipped under his bowtie and he tugs it off. Next, he slides off his jacket and unbuttons his shirt, exposing the lean, defined torso beneath it. Curling tattoos wrap around his abdomen and up over his chest. I can't help but reach out and touch them—a deadly looking tiger clashes with an unfurling flower, meeting a series of dates and a quote scrawled in what looks like someone's handwriting.

"Like what you see?" He asks, low in his throat, as he slides his shirt off. I smile and tip my chin at him.

"Not half bad," I say, and he scoffs before leaning down and kissing me hard.

"You have a smart mouth for someone who's talking to her boss right now," he murmurs into my mouth. I laugh, head tipped back, but my laughter dissolves into a gasp when one of his hands slides up my body and grazes over my breast.

"Is this okay?" He asks, and it takes me a moment to find my breath, to push the word past my lips.

"Yes," I breathe, arching into his touch.

"More?"

"Yes."

His hands ease the straps of my dress down my shoulders, leaving trailing heat on my skin as they brush over it.

"Jesus," he says roughly. "You're incredible."

He kisses down my throat and over my collarbone until his lips are brushing the thin lace of my bra. I thread my fingers through his hair, holding him closer to me, needing to feel him on every inch of my skin. He brushes a thumb over one of my nipples. The touch is like electricity—I feel it in every nerve, all the way down to my toes.

"Please," I say, my voice breaking.

Alec kisses me again, his tongue dancing against mine. I can feel him smiling into the kiss. "Can I take this off?" He asks, hands brushing over my dress as he moves down my neck again, biting down on the tender skin there. I know I'll leave this place with a bruise, a problem for a later time. I nod and sit up as he turns me around, reaching for the zipper and sliding it down with agonizing slowness. He kisses my neck as he pushes the dress down to my hips, and it takes a monumental effort for me to keep myself together as I slide it the rest of the way off.

Then we're falling into each other again, his hands so hot on my waist and my hips. I can feel how hard he is against my thigh, and it makes my heart pound, makes my body arch up into him even more.

We shouldn't be doing this, I think, back to his words from earlier. I know it's foolish. I know that maybe later, I'll regret getting myself into a situation like this. But I think if he stopped touching me right now, I might die.

"Not fair," I say breathlessly, "I'm nearly naked and you still have your pants on."

Alec unhooks my bra and leaves me in nothing but my underwear. He runs a thumb over one nipple again while he focuses his mouth on the other, his teeth grazing me and making my eyelids flutter. The sensation is nearly too much to bear. I gasp as he touches me, until finally he pulls back to unzip his pants and tosses them somewhere unseen on the floor. His dark briefs blend into the artwork of his tattoos as they continue down his thighs, wrapping around the muscle and emphasizing the linework of his veins and his strength.

He takes his time working his way up my body, hands leaving fiery trails along my thighs as he holds them tight to his waist, his fingers curling into skin hard enough to leave bruises in their wake. But in comparison his kisses are languid, almost gentle. It makes me feel overwhelmed with desire, crazy for him, needing more. I curl my hands at the nape of his neck and drag my nails through his hair, gasping as he sucks another mark into the column of my throat. A hand moves to cup my breast and he curses under his breath.

"How can someone be this beautiful?" He murmurs. "The things you're doing to me should be illegal."

In response, I grind my thigh against the hardness straining his briefs. He hisses, and I try to ignore the way it makes my stomach flip with butterflies.

"I want you," he says roughly. "Now."

I dare him with my eyes. "Then take me."

He tugs my underwear down with one strong hand and then his fingers are gentle again, trailing down over me before he slides one inside of my heat.

I gasp, head tipping back, the sensation nearly enough to make me see stars. He crooks that finger inside of me and I feel him grin against my neck.

"Good?" He asks, and I want to say yes, yes, it's everything, it's more than good, but all I can do is gasp and nod in response. His hands are masterful—a thumb presses against my sex as he adds another finger inside of me, working me open and making me moan.

"Please, Alec," I gasp, running a hand down his back, gliding my nails over his warm skin. He groans against my shoulder, and a thrill runs through me at the sound, the thought that we can both make each other feel so overwhelmed enough to bring me closer to the edge.

"Wait, wait," I say, pushing gently at his shoulder and he looks up, pulling his hands away from me.

"What's wrong?"

"Nothing, I just—" I gasp at the absence of his fingers. "I'm close and I want you inside of me."

He grins, eyes dark and heavy. He rises to his knees and slides off his briefs. My mouth nearly waters at the sight of him kneeling over me like this, naked and strong, his body defined and wanting. I trace my eyes down the length of him, to his hard member. It feels like a matter of seconds pass before he's feeling for a condom in the table beside his bed and rolling it on, the whole time keeping his eyes trained on me. I thought I would feel nervous or insecure, splayed out like this in front of him, but I'm only flushed with excitement.

He kisses me as he slides into me and I cry out into his mouth, gasping, begging him for more. There's no slow start, nothing gentle now—he fucks into me hard, desperation clear in the way he pants my name beside my ear. I feel like I'm part of him as he reaches for the headboard and rolls his hips up to meet mine, his lips pressed against my shoulder, his back muscles moving beneath my hands.

"Thalia," he gasps against my skin.

He doesn't have to say it. I can feel it in the way he thrusts into me, in the desperation in his voice. "Me too," I say, "I'm so close."

Just a few more snaps of his hips and we're both moaning against each other, coming at once. I blink back stars as his hips stutter inside of me. There's a moment of pure bliss, white spots trailing at the edges of my vision, both of us hot and sticky but sated.

I keep running a hand through his hair, not wanting him far from me. But he finally pulls out with a groan and pulls me into his arms.

"I can't believe we did that," I say with a little laugh.

He grins against my neck. His arms trace lazy circles over my back and my hip.

"Me neither," Alec says. His voice is rough and breathless. I cup his cheek and kiss him and he presses me back down into the pillows, kissing me back, hard.

"You're incredible," he says softly. "I can't thank you enough. For, you know, everything, but especially...this."

Alec rises and retrieves a washcloth to clean us both up. I sigh at the loss of his warmth but he's back quickly, cleaning me up, a small smile on his face. His hands draw lines across my waist, pinning me in place. I smile up at him. "You know, if I thought this was how our first event might end, I would have applied for the job much earlier."

Alec laughs and slides back into the bed with me. "And I wouldn't have been the idiot who said that we shouldn't hire you."

"That's old news by now," I say with a sated sigh, curling into him, savoring his touch. He's so warm, so strong, so perfectly fitted against me. He pulls me into his front, little spoon, and presses his mouth against my ear.

"Rest," he says. "I'll be here when you wake up."

And I trust him when he says it, so I let my eyes drift shut, with Alec holding me through the night.

# Chapter Eleven

Alec

I wake to sun coming through the blinds in my bedroom, feeling like the luckiest man on earth. Thalia is curled up beside me, still naked, the sun painting stripes across her back. She looks so beautiful—even with her hair mussed and her face slack in sleep, she's angelic, as if someone painted her to hang above their mantle.

I rub her back with feather-light fingers, trying not to wake her but wanting to touch her. I still can't believe that it's real. That I really had sex with my employee. With my fake girlfriend, who apparently is a lot closer to the real thing than I had once believed.

The thought is terrifying. I haven't been with anyone in years. At least, not until last night. I've never had luck in relationships, especially not with people I work with, and not with rich girls with high society families. What would they think if they could see me, the perfect combination of all their worst fears in a future partner for their daughter?

Maybe I made a stupid mistake. Maybe we should have never done this, just left things as they were, let the tension build until eventually one of us had to go.

But then Thalia stirs in her sleep and turns to face me, a sleepy smile on her face. "Hey handsome," she says, and the soft lull of her voice after waking is enough to banish all of my anxieties.

"Hi beautiful," I answer low in my throat, and I lean in to kiss her, not caring about morning breath or what I must look like—spent, half-asleep, unshaven. She sighs happily against my mouth, and I cup a hand over her smooth waist, savoring the curves I find there.

"We need to get up," Thalia says, but her eyes are half-shut, her lips quirked in a satisfied smirk.

"It's a Saturday," I groan.

"Aren't you the one who told me weekends are just for working harder? Besides, I take a Saturday class so I can finish my degree early—some of us still have to show up," she says with a little laugh.

I kiss her again instead of answering, because I want to ignore the world a little longer, keep my eyes on her and her only. But we're interrupted by the chime of her phone, an incessant noise that tears a groan from me.

Thalia sighs and sits up to look at it. Her eyebrows raise as she reads whatever she's seeing.

"Tell me," I say, propping my head up on an arm. I appreciate the way her eyes travel across my bicep and the artwork that intertwines there before she can answer.

"It's Megan, she posted the photo from last night. It's already blowing up—there are thousands of comments."

"Good for them," I answer, rolling onto my back with a sigh.

Thalia's eyes narrow. "God, there are some awful comments on here. And they're all from anonymous accounts."

"Cowards," I growl. "People are always going to be hateful, especially if I'm involved." I turn to her and rest my hand against her waist, savoring the warmth of her bare skin under my palm. "Don't let them get to you."

"I'm not," she answers quickly, almost too quickly, but she kisses me again before I have a chance to call her out on the lie. "I really do have to get ready for class, though. And you have to go to the office and start purchasing guitars."

She's right, I almost forgot. We'll finally be able to put those donations to good use.

"Fine," I say, eyes half shut, already settling back into the bed. She playfully shoves my shoulder.

"Come on, don't make me do a walk of shame out of your apartment. Besides, you drove me here—I'll need a ride to campus."

That idea gets me out of bed. I wonder what it will be like, pulling up to her campus in my car and letting her out in front of all those people. Showing them who she belongs to. Who she chose.

We make breakfast together, just simple eggs fried in the pan with toast and bacon. I let her borrow a shirt and it nearly drowns her, the black button down stark against her warm honey skin. I end up kissing her against the kitchen counter while the bacon sizzles in the pan, unable to keep my hands off her. I can't believe this hold she has on me—it makes me feel crazed, hungry for something that no meal could ever satisfy.

When it's time to go, the coffee finished and breakfast just scraps on my ceramic plates, Thalia fishes in her bag and pulls out a skirt that she zips into place over my shirt, managing to turn the outfit into something sophisticated and sleek.

"What did you have that for?" I ask, smirking as I run a hand over her waist. "Were you planning to spend the night with me?"

"You wish," Thalia says with a wicked glint in her eyes. "I wasn't sure what it would be like, after the party. I wanted to be prepared to change out of that ridiculous dress if I needed to."

"Smart girl," I say, and the words are muffled against her mouth as we kiss again, long and languid, unwilling to break apart. But I can feel my phone buzzing in my pocket and Thalia taps two fingers against the hand I have on her waist.

"Class time," she says in a sing-songy voice.

I relent, and let her slip from my grasp.

I drive over to the campus, sun hot overhead and summer in the air. Birds call high overhead among the tops of palm trees, and everything feels bright, vivid, hopeful. I feel lighter. I didn't realize how much I needed this—a successful night and someone by my side who believes in me wholeheartedly. I don't think I even realized that it was possible to have someone like that who wasn't just an employee, but someone who went beyond the confines of the walls I had built.

It's a scary feeling, to be vulnerable and open. But what did closing myself off ever get me? Only pain and isolation.

"Thanks for the ride," Thalia says as we pull up. She turns to me and smiles, though something falters at the corner of her lips when I lean in to kiss her.

"What's wrong?" I ask, a breath away.

"I was just thinking, do you mind if we...don't mention anything about last night in the office? I already got a few judging glares from people around Sound Connections just for the pictures we posted on social, and most of them likely don't realize that they were staged. I just don't want everyone to think I'm trying to take advantage of you or wanting to sleep my way to the top."

"Who's being rude to you?" I asked, feeling immediately protective of her. She laughs softly and cups my cheek with her hand.

"No one, forget it. I'm just saying that it's different when you're new and a girl and suddenly you're, um, having relations with your boss. It looks awful. People talk."

I grimace, but I can see where she's coming from. I'm not ashamed of what we've done, but I don't expect everyone to understand it either.

"We won't say a word," I affirm, and I love the way her face lights up with a reassured smile.

"Okay," she says.

"Okay," I answer, and both of us hover in the car, neither wanting the other to go.

"I guess I'll see you this afternoon then," she says at last, and then she slips from the car with a fast peck on my lips and a little wave. I watch her walk away until she disappears past the doors of the main hall.

Fuck. One night and I'm already in too deep.

I head over to the office, preparing myself for Megan's over the top enthusiasm at last night events. Instead, I walk into the front door and find her waiting by the entry desk, her expression ashen.

"Have you checked your socials?" She asks quickly.

"Not yet," I say. "But Thalia checked this morning, and showed me that she had gotten some hate comments. Why? What's up?"

"There's something you need to know. Can we go to your office?"

Worry starts to stir inside of me, fast and intense as birds in a cage. "Fine. Lead the way."

Megan hurries to my office and shuts the door behind us once we're inside. "Someone leaked the fact that you two aren't actually dating. It must have happened last night at the event."

"Then deny it," I say, face heating up with a mix of anger and nerves. I hate being in the spotlight for anything—people always use it as an excuse to talk about how they know I'm a bad person, how they can just tell by the way that I look. It's all bullshit.

"They have a source, Alec, saying that they heard the whole thing was a publicity stunt. It would look awful for us to just deny it with no proof."

"Don't we have proof? The nights we went out to dinner and the garden date?"

"They're not solid. The photographers could stab us in the back and sell more information." Megan sighs, running a hand over her face in exasperation. "I'm sorry, Alec. I don't know who could have possibly started this mess."

"Well, I need you to find out. Now. And then I need you to do damage control, and fix this whole thing as soon as possible."

"On it, boss," Megan says with a frown on her face. "Hey, did you say Thalia showed you the comments this morning? Were you with her?"

I school my face into a stone cold expression, but Megan knows me too well to believe it. "Alec, don't tell me you two..."

"Don't you have work that needs to get done?"

Megan sighs. "Alec, I need to know what's going on if I'm going to do my job properly. Are you two hooking up?"

I feel my face heat up. I don't know why I'm embarrassed, but sometimes with Megan it feels like I'm talking to a sister, and I don't exactly want to tell my sister who I'm having sex with.

"Yes," I finally admit, expression sour.

"Jesus. Okay, good to know. Hell, maybe that will work out in our favor in this whole mess. I'll get back to you when I have updates."

And with that said, she disappears from my office in a huff.

I sit down at the desk, feeling flustered and shocked. Who would have told? Who knows beside myself, Thalia, and Megan? Could one of those photographers sold us out based on the little information Megan provided them with? And why? Just to stir up gossip?

A sickly feeling pools in my stomach as I remember something from the night before—Thalia walking with Matthew Torres down that winding path, and the way she froze up when I spotted them together. No. She wouldn't have done that. She wouldn't risk ruining her own career and reputation just to get on Torres's good side, would she?

Thalia is a good person. She believes in Sound Connections.

But what if Torres made her an offer? If she helped him take down our company, maybe he'd give her a better position, higher pay, a name in the tabloids that wasn't connected to a relationship or her parents. He's always hated me, and it wouldn't shock me if he tried to pull her over to his business.

But it would shock me if she had accepted.

Rage coils inside of me, though I don't even know who it's aimed at. But I promise myself—I will find out.

# Chapter Twelve

Thalia

Class runs late, and I have to catch a ride with my friend Lauren from our Sociology class to Sound Connections. She spends the whole ride telling me about her own experience on the app, where she met a boy who only listened to songs from movie soundtracks, and how that relationship made her never believe in love again. But I can barely hear her—all I can think about is Alec, how his scent still clings to my clothes and my hair, his shirt loose and comfortable around me, his mouth the sweetest thing I'd tasted in years.

"Thanks for the ride," I tell Lauren as she drops me off with a wide smile and a request to tell Alec she's a big fan of what his business is doing. I promise to get coffee with her someday soon and hurry into the office, already five minutes past our start time.

Inside, everything is frantic. There are people on the phone, people taking notes, people running back and forth. I weave through the mess, trying to avoid the suspicious glances I get in the process, and make my way to Alec's office.

I knock quickly and shut the door behind me after he answers. But Alec barely looks up from his computer, his expression just a series of hard lines, his body language taut and stressed.

"Hi," I breathe, "sorry I'm late."

I want to go to him, want to slide into his lap and feel his hands running over my spine and cupping my thighs. But there's something off—what could have possibly changed in the past few hours?

"Been on your phone recently?" He asks, voice cold.

"No," I answer quickly. I fish my phone out of my pocket and start scrolling, my hands nearly shaking. It doesn't take long to find what he's talking about.

LOVE CONNECTION FRAUD? Alec Lynch of Sound Connections is pretending to date Malibu Mayor candidate's daughter—also his employee!

"What is this?" I ask, jaw dropping. "Who told them to publish this?"

"I was going to ask you the same thing."

He finally looks at me, and his eyes are ice cold. "What were you and Matthew Torres really talking about last night, Thalia?"

My blood runs cold. "You can't possibly think—"

My mind runs back through the events of the night before. I had started to walk out of the banquet hall, feet hurting and my whole body ready for sleep, when Torres had run up and called my name. We walked together down the path as he spoke. He asked how long Alec and I had been together, and told me that he thought we made a great match. But the whole time he spoke, he had seemed haughty, like he knew something he shouldn't. Could he have heard something we said during the event? Sold us out to the press?

"I didn't say a word to Matthew Torres," I insist.

"I find that hard to believe," Alec snaps. "This has him written all over it. He's been trying to run this little smear campaign against Sound Connections for years, and you're the one who had isolated contact with him last night. Who else could have told him?"

My heart is racing as panic washes over me. I start to doubt my own words, my own memories. Could I have said the wrong thing? Made him think that we weren't truly together?

No, I know that this wasn't me. I'm good at talking to people, and I've faked enough smiles in a lifetime to know that Matthew Torres would never be able to trick me into opening up to him.

"I can't believe you would accuse me," I say softly, horror dawning on my face. But Alec's expression doesn't soften.

"Well, I barely know you, do I Thalia?"

The words are like a stake to the heart. I falter, my hands knotting in front of me, like they were trying to reach for him and found themselves frozen halfway through the process.

"Go home for the day," he says finally, his voice clipped.

Anger fills me—I want to lash out, prove him wrong, tell him that he's an idiot for even considering that I could do something like that.

"Are you serious right now?" I say, my fury trembling through my voice. "Alec, you know that I—"

"It's Mr. Lynch," he snaps. "We need to be professional here. Don't know who's listening, do we?"

I feel tears prickle at the corners of my eyes. I can't believe I managed to forget how cold he could be to me in a matter of hours, as if last night meant nothing to him.

"Got it, Mr. Lynch," I say, ice in my voice. I turn to grab the doorknob and leave his office without a second glance. I'm not going to stand here and be reprimanded for something that I didn't do.

"Megan told me that the school is upset about the press we're surrounding them with," he says to my back, his voice so even and clipped that it strikes fear in my heart. "They're considering not even accepting the donation. Do you understand the repercussions of this now?"

My hand trembles on the knob. I want to turn around and give him a piece of my mind. But now, he's knocked me down to nothing, and I regret even coming in today.

I leave the room and close the door quietly behind me.

I hurry down the hall, hoping that I can make it to the bathroom before I can burst into tears, but Megan catches me in the hallway.

"Thalia," she breathes, "I don't know if Alec already told you, but you need to—"

"Sorry, I need to go," I say in a flash, shrugging off the hand she rests on my shoulder. I barely make it out of the building before I burst into tears. I sit behind the wheel of my car and cry until I know my mascara is leaving dark tracks down my cheeks.

When I get home, my mother is in the kitchen, stirring a cup of tea. She looks up with furrowed eyebrows when I walk into the room. "Thalia? What's wrong, honey?"

"I thought you were at work," I say, my voice thick. But instead of answering, she just pulls me into a hug. That makes me break down all over again—my mother has never been very affectionate, always too busy to consider the emotions she thought to be frivolous. But now, all I can think about is how grateful I am to be held by her, comforted in the aftermath of my stupidity.

"I took time off, I had a migraine. The tea is helping though. Now what's this about, darling?" She asks against my hair.

I lean against her shoulder. "I just—I messed up at work."

"Is this about that man you're working for? What did he do?"

"It's not like that, Mother, I just—" It feels too intimidating to say it out loud. I don't want her view of me to change, for her to think that I'm a mess just because I went along with this entire plan. "It was just a bad day."

She runs a hand over my hair, comforting me in a way that I've wanted for a long time. It makes me feel like a kid again to be like this with her.

"I'm sorry, darling. You should just rest tonight, sleep in and take care of yourself. And you know, you never have to go back to that place if you don't want to. Your father has a position always waiting for you, whenever you need it. Don't waste time with people who don't value who you are."

For the first time in a long time, her lecture gets to me—maybe she's right. Maybe I don't need this, any of this. Maybe I'd be better off just doing what I was raised to do. Pleasing my parents and making progress in the political world, like the daughter I was born to be.

But I don't answer her. I just let her hug me until it's too much and then I go to my room, shutting my phone off so that I don't have to see the comments and articles advertising what a mess I am. If my mother checks the local tabloids, maybe she'll learn all about it—the embarrassment that her daughter is.

It takes everything in me not to cry again. Instead, I just fall asleep with the lights still on, unable to even rouse myself to try and pull myself together.

If Alec wants to blame all his problems on me, then he can do that. I know who I am and what I'm capable of, and I'm not going to let him walk all over me, especially not after how...vulnerable I was with him.

When Monday comes, I'll show him exactly who he hired. And I won't let him forget it.

# Chapter Thirteen

Alec

Megan tells me to take the rest of the weekend to cool down. She promises that she's got it—she'll figure out exactly what's going on and hold whoever spread our secret accountable.

But when I step back into the office on Monday morning, the energy is still frantic. Damage control seems to permeate every department of Sound Connections. Already my phone has blown up with notifications—statements saying that the claims are "obviously false," without much evidence beside the staged photos of Thalia and I. The whole thing nearly pushes me over the edge into a sickening mix of fury and humiliation.

But I handle it how I would any other problem—by shutting myself in my office and ignoring it in favor of trying to do something actually productive. I spend the morning focusing on the donations, doling out what money will go toward instruments, what might be beneficial for bus trips around the state for competitions. It's easy to lose myself in my work, and I find myself ignoring many of the knocks on my door, preferring to stay cut off from whatever mess is happening past my office. This whole thing was Megan's idea anyway—why should I have to clean up a mess that I didn't want to be a part of in the first place?

My mind drifts, thinking back to the night after the benefit. My hands remember Thalia—her smooth curves, her warm mouth against mine, full lips kissing back with desperation. I've never been with a person who made me feel like that, so full of fire and desire and emotions that I had never been able to put words to in the past.

Finally, as the afternoon rolls around and I've had about five cups of coffee, Megan opens my office door without knocking. Thalia is standing beside her, face carved out of stone, completely cold. I feel hurt and angry for a moment, and then I force myself to clear my mind. To cut off the feelings. To remember that this woman might have pulled me into her, but she was ready to throw me under the bus the whole time.

"We're coming in," Megan says bluntly, before I can deny her. She slips in and shuts the door behind her and Thalia. "We need to talk, Alec."

"About what?" I say coldly. "I thought we already spoke about this."

"About the two of you," Megan bites back. "I know you're not happy, and I apologize for the mess." She sits in one of the chairs across from me and gestures to Thalia to sit in the other one. When Thalia finally does, Megan leans back and crosses her arms over her chest. "Yes, it's a disaster. Yes, we had to do major damage control. But downloads for Sound Connections are at record highs. And once this whole thing passes, people will forget all about the negatives and will only remember your name."

I scoff. "I find that hard to believe."

Thalia is silent. Her eyes look red around the edges but her mouth is set in a hard, unfeeling line. I try not to think about the way her lips had parted as I touched her. I try not to remember the heat of her body against mine, and how special it had felt with her in my arms, coming alive all around me.

"Trust me," Megan says at last, after a beat of silence.

"All I do is trust you, Meg. It's everyone else that I have to worry about." I glare in Thalia's direction when I say this, trying to control my anger but feeling the betrayal burn fire-hot in my chest. Megan sighs and runs a hand over her face.

"I don't know if people are going to believe the denials we've sent to the press," Megan says. "It wouldn't be the end of the world if they didn't, but we'll have extreme damage control to do with Malibu High and the donors who came to Friday's event. But I have a different idea."

"Then feel free to share with the class," I say, trying not to sound as bitter as I'm feeling.

"We need to stage a breakup."

"Excuse me?" Thalia and I both say at once, her voice high and thin, mine low and incredulous.

"Won't that just put the spotlight on us again?" I ask. I cross my arms over my chest with a frown.

"There's no way we can continue to pretend you two are dating without people continuously asking questions," Megan says with a sigh. "It will be better just to cut it off quickly and do damage control later on. Trust me."

What if it isn't pretend? I want to say, but the words are foolish, something a kid would say just because he's afraid of what's going to happen next. But the thought nags at me. What if we were real?

"Fine with me," Thalia says under her breath, and the words twist in my gut, bringing red to the corners of my vision all over again.

"Fine then," I say, agreeing even as the words turn to acid in my mouth. If Thalia wants nothing to do with me, then that's how this will be. I'm not the one who threw both of us under the bus. I have nothing to apologize for.

"Fine," Megan says, a smarmy smirk on her lips, like she thinks she knows what's going on behind the scenes here. But if I could be honest with her, I know she'd be stunned—she has no idea the truth of what Thalia and I are. Or, I guess, were.

"Good," she says again, when neither of us speak up. "Well, we'll orchestrate the whole thing on your account Alec. We'll tell everyone that the rumors and speculation pushed you two to break up—maybe that will guilt these vultures enough to leave you alone for a while. Stay off social media for the next couple of days while this blows over."

"You don't have to tell me twice," I mutter. Thalia won't look at me. Megan stands up to leave and calls to Thalia but receives only a shake of the head as a response.

"I need to speak with Alec alone," Thalia says, her voice still firm and cold. Megan blinks in surprise but nods and leaves, closing the door tightly behind her.

"There's nothing to say," I respond, turning back to my computer. But Thalia just clears her throat.

"I don't think it's right for me to continue working here," she says. Her voice trembles around the last word. This gets my attention—I turn to her and focus my gaze on her frozen face, the emotion behind her eyes tightly guarded.

"What are you talking about?" I ask, my voice rough.

"Why would I stay somewhere where I'm clearly not welcome?" She says, her tone rising as she continues. "You don't need me—that much is clear. It would make more sense for me to quit and for us both to go about our lives."

I can't argue with her, but despite my apprehension and rage at being sold out to the media by her, a huge part of me wants to cling to her, to tell her to stop being ridiculous and to get back to work. But after knowing her, I can tell by the look in her eyes that she means it. I can't remember a time in my life when I didn't know Thalia, and that's a thought that scares me. I don't want to be this person who relies on others to feel stable and happy.

When I was a kid, I found all my joy in the friends I made. My parents didn't understand or respect me—they thought I was a lost cause. When I started to fail classes, deciding instead to spend my days causing trouble with my friends, smoking and drinking and playing music in their basements, my parents didn't ask me what was wrong. They took one look at me and declared me a mistake; they didn't want to dirty their hands with me. It took years for me to move past that pain. The two people in the world that were supposed to love me unconditionally wanted nothing to do with me and thought I was a disgrace. As a result, I failed out of school and couch hopped for years, starting unsuccessful bands, drinking too much, and spending all my money on tattoos. It was stupid. I know that now. But the people I met along the way supported me so much more than my so called "family" ever did.

I had to rely on someone to get by—so I relied on my friends. And over the years, as they stayed stagnant in the lives that they enjoyed, I knew I needed to change, needed to become the kind of man who didn't need anyone to be happy. That mindset led to years of failed relationships and lonely nights, until I was finally able to pitch Sound Connections and make it a reality with the support of a few of my high school teachers, the only people who ever thought I might be worth something.

I thought maybe that Thalia could be a person like that—someone who, despite their upbringing, saw me as a real person, with thoughts and feelings and goals and intelligence. She never made me feel stupid, never tore me down, only did whatever she could to improve my life and business. And the time we spent together made me realize that I had never felt like that about someone else before—not once, not ever.

And then she stabbed me in the back. Here she is, twisting the knife.

"It will be for the better," Thalia says, her voice broken. "For both of us. Thank you for your time and assistance, Alec. I wish you the best."

And before I can find the words to say anything—no, wait, stop, we need you here, I need you, I just want to understand why you did it—she's leaving my office and shutting the door behind her.

I sit in my chair for a long moment, watching the wood grain on the back of the heavy door, wishing I could bring myself to get to my feet and tell her to come back here and tell me the truth so we can move past this once and for all.

But I'm frozen. And by the time I can force myself to get to my feet, she's gone, the hallway just full of milling interns who give me timid smiles.

I go back to work, and try to forget I ever knew Thalia Weaver.

# Chapter Fourteen

Thalia

I made the only choice I had. I took myself out of the equation before anyone else could get hurt.

I know myself well enough by now to know when I have feelings for someone—and as soon as I stepped into Alec's office, I knew that it was over for me. He looked so gorgeous, even full of anger and spite for me. His hair was as dark and lovely as ever, falling in his deep blue eyes, highlighting the shadows of his jawbone.

But as I took the seat across from him and knew deep in my heart that I had to put distance between us. I could still feel the sparks, the undying heat in me that begged to be closer, to cross the room and straddle his lap and pull his mouth up to meet mine.

So I quit.

That evening, I send Megan an email, outlining the details of my estrangement from Sound Connections.

Thanks for the time we spent together, Megan, I say. I learned a lot from you in our short interactions and I'm grateful that I had the chance to work with you. But unfortunately, this isn't going to work out for me as a continued position. I wish you the best.

I hit send before I have a chance to question what I'm doing. I'm making the right choice, I tell myself. I have to do this. There's no other option.

I go home that night and find myself crying again, the house empty, my parents off at some dinner party with their friends. I never realized how lonely the whole place could feel, but after spending time in Alec's intimate apartment and filling my days with thoughts of him and Sound Connections, the loss of it all feels so abrupt.

The next few days are busy with just my thoughts and the blocks I set up on all my social media. I don't want to see the posts that Megan shares through Alec's account—even if I know he's not really the one making the statements, it still hurts just as much to consider him talking about separating himself from me.

My mother tries to bring it up after hearing about the breakup—but I can't talk about it, especially not with her. Instead, I give myself a few days to mope and then I find my dad one evening after he's coming home from a day of work.

"Dad," I say as I spot him in his den, feet kicked up on the coffee table as the TV hums at a quiet volume. "Can I talk to you?"

He leans his head back, eyes shut. "What is it Thalia? I'm exhausted."

"I want to work with you on the campaign."

He blinks his eyes open and smiles at me. "Really? Wow, I'm so glad to hear that honey. You really mean it?"

I nod, smiling, though my stomach feels like it's turning sour.

"Amazing! You can come into the office with me tomorrow. We have a team of interns working on our social presence right now, trying to stir up the vote and build a team for canvassing. It's hard work, honey, but I think you're really going to have a great time. You'll learn so much for your own political career."

His words are as firm as a punch to the gut but I nod along, keeping the smile plastered on my face. This is fine. Everything is fine. The nonprofit work is done, in the past, just something that will one day be a distant memory. My future is in this moment—in the time that I take my dad up on his offer and become the child that they both expected me to be.

Early the next morning, he urges me to skip class and attend a meeting where his team will discuss what neighborhoods need him the most. Everyone in the conference room looks like the type of person my parents always expected me to be—well dressed, smiling, blond and bright and oozing wealth. They all clearly are there for a reason—they want to see my dad as the next mayor, because they know he's here to support people who live lives like them.

And despite the years of benefiting from a life like that, I can't seem to agree with them. I know how lucky I was to grow up with rich parents—I never wanted for anything, always given the best of the best, food on the table and opportunities in every direction. But I wanted to be free of them all the while. I wanted to make choices for myself. I wanted to do good for the world. Is that so wrong, to want to break free from the life they constructed for me and change someone else's along the way?

I thought that maybe I had found a kindred spirit when it came to Alec—someone who understood me and my goals with aspirations of his own becoming tangible.

But now, looking around the conference room, everyone's words and voices rising around me and speaking over me and turning my mind to mush, I think that maybe I was wrong. There is no way for me to break out of this path—it was always going to be like this, with me sitting here in my father's office, trying to help him climb the ladder of success so that maybe one day I could have a life of my own, too.

I spend the whole day after the group meeting doing grunt work for the office. I run to get coffees, drop off mail, and organize papers for people on the campaign, all while brainstorming ideas for their social campaign. It's not much different from the work I would have done at Sound Connections if I could have stayed, but for some reason it feels so much worse. I don't feel like I belong here, among these ivy league students who look at my father like he's the kind of man who could be a god. They want to be just like him—handsome, rich, successful. They don't care what it takes to get there, or who might suffer.

By the end of the day, I'm exhausted, and I still have assignments that need to be done for class the next day. But all I want to do is go home and sleep until my thoughts are erased from my mind. Instead, I climb into my car and nearly jump out of my skin when I hear my phone start to ring. I check it and spot Megan's number. My stomach sinks all the way to the floor.

"Hello?" I say.

"Thalia, what the hell is going on?" Megan asks as soon as I answer. "Alec tells me that you quit—is that true?"

I swallow, hard. The feeling pools in my stomach along with jitters of anxiety in my veins. "Yes, it is true," I answer.

"Well why the hell would you do something like that?" Megan scoffed, confusion intertwined with her voice.

"Didn't he tell you? Alec thinks I'm the one who leaked...you know, everything."

Megan makes a noise of surprise. "Well, did you?"

I blink in surprise at the genuine question in her voice.

"No, no. Of course not."

"Good. I didn't think you would have done something like that, especially not at the cost of your own job." Megan takes a deep, shaking breath. "Listen, Thalia, between us...Alec can truly be an idiot sometimes. He's not used to people caring for him or trying to help him in any way. It took years of me working for him to convince him that I was truly here to help, not to tear him down. I'm not trying to make excuses for him, but I just want you to see where he's coming from. Don't give up on him yet. Just let me...clean up this mess."

I sigh, leaning and pressing my forehead against the steering wheel of my car. The evening settles around me as people leave the office and head home. I keep the phone pressed to my ear, Megan on the other end of the line.

"Promise, Thalia? You're the first person I've seen him happy around in a long time. Don't lose faith. I know there has to been an answer to this mess, and we'll hold whoever it was accountable—but don't beat yourself up over something that wasn't your fault."

I squeeze my eyes shut. "Fine, just—just keep me updated, okay? I can't be around him right now. It's just a difficult situation, and I've already accepted a new internship."

Megan sighs. "Do whatever you need to do, kid. I'll be here."

She hangs up after saying goodbye and I stay where I am for a long moment, unable to force myself to pick my head up and drive home. I know exactly where I have to go. I know exactly what I have to do. But all I want right now is to take the winding highways back to Alec's place and fall into his bed with him, to forget about everything that has happened in the past few days and feel his touch.

Instead, I shift the car into drive, and I pull away into the setting sun, heading for home.

# Chapter Fifteen

Alec

"It's wonderful to speak with you again, Mr. Lynch," the interviewer says as she takes the seat across from me in the conference room.

"Likewise," I answer, though I can't remember ever meeting this woman before, and this is the last place that I want to be right now. My suit feels uncomfortably tight and hot around my arms. The room is too warm, the lights too bright, and all I want right now is to go back to bed.

Megan scheduled this interview a few days ago, against my protests. She said it would be beneficial for me to speak to someone, to get my voice out there, to prevent the rumors from popping up and making everything a hundred times worse. But I don't care what these people say about me. It's all just a waste of my time in the end, just like my days with Thalia, just like the betrayal where she stabbed me in the back.

"You've been a hot topic lately," the interviewer says with a bright smile, interrupting my thoughts. I can't remember her name—Jamie? Jessica? She looks like a Jessica, bubbly, bright, dressed in vivid colors. "We're so thankful that you decided to sit down with our publication and share your story—every girl in Malibu is dying to know if you're an eligible bachelor once again."

I scoff, a sound that Megan shows me is clearly not approved by her narrowed eyes and protruding frown. I shrug, trying to compose myself once again.

"Well, it's not exactly a secret anymore, is it?" I sit up in my seat and cross my arms over my chest. "Thalia is a great girl, but these rumors about our whole relationship being faked really scared her. It's not like I'm some celebrity, you know? I'm just a man trying to make my way in this industry. I don't want to be followed by paparazzi and held up to some strange standard. I want to be myself and date who I want and not bring people down along the way.

Jessica? Nods along with what I'm saying, a smarmy smile on her face. "I can't even imagine how you must be struggling. Our sources had some truly wicked things to say about the two of you—they said they attended your benefit dinner the other day and pointed out how uncomfortable you two looked together, like you'd been forced to pose for pictures."

I grind my teeth together, trying to keep myself contained and professional. Megan narrows her eyes at me. I can feel her pleading with me, begging me to keep it all together.

They were at the event, I think, seething. If it wasn't Thalia, who would it be?

Then another thought pops into my mind, sabotaging my own ideas. She was uncomfortable around you. She spread this rumor so she could get away from you.

And that idea sends chills down my spine, a sudden and swift sick feeling twisting in my stomach. Maybe she hated being around me so much that she felt this was her only option.

"Being in the public eye would be uncomfortable for anyone," I say at last, when I notice that Megan is waving her hand and encouraging me to answer the question. "Thalia is relatively new to this field, and was just starting to get used to attending events with me. It's hardly fair to judge her comfort at a huge event like the benefit."

Jessica? Sighs in agreement, nodding along yet again. "So true, Mr. Lynch. I can definitely see where you're coming from and I'm sorry to hear that this has been a tough adjustment for the two of you. But I also have to point out that your fans and followers are suffering now—you and Thalia were the perfect example of a success story when it came to Sound Connections. People want to see love bloom like it did on your app, and they loved hearing that you two were together."

She holds up her phone, focusing on an Instagram post of the two of us in a garden, hundreds of comments splayed out beneath it. "This relationship announcement was the highlight of so many Sound Connections users' experience. What do you have to say to the people who think love might be dead?"

They're right, I want to say. Love is just a construct—just an idea we made to make ourselves feel better, just a mechanism to defend from our own loneliness. I thought that for a moment maybe I could like Thalia—maybe I could even grow to feel more strongly about her than I've ever felt about another person. But she was just using me to push herself along, wasn't she?

"I think it's all about luck," I say at last, my voice rough and laced with pain. "I was lucky to have some time with Thalia, and I enjoyed our experience together. Love is out there, and Sound Connections users know that without my relationship as a point of reference. They have so much proof in their own meetups and relationships."

Jessica? Looks skeptical but she nods with a wide smile. "That's great to hear, Mr. Lynch. How do you feel about the allegations Matthew Torres made recently about your company duplicating a design that his app, Songbird, also implemented?"

I scowl. I can't help it—it's instinct for Torres's name to sour my mood. I shrug, trying to pass off the emotion, but I can't help the awful feeling that curls in my gut, like a warning sign for danger I haven't yet discovered.

"Matthew Torres enjoys running his mouth," I snap back, and I ignore Megan as she runs an exasperated hand down her face, clearly overwhelmed by what I have to say. But it's the truth, and I'm not going to let him get away with shitting on my business just because his dad won't bail him out of his failures anymore. "Torres needs to focus more on his numbers, and not what Sound Connections is doing. Our interface is entirely unique and hasn't used any of the technology from

Songbird—if they disagree, they can bring it up with me, and we can have a real discussion about it."

The interviewer raises her eyebrows at me, but the wicked smile on her face shows me that she's enjoying every moment of this. I smile back, and I put every ounce of venom I feel in the expression.

"You're an interesting man, Mr. Lynch," she says with a satisfied look on her face. "Thank you for taking the time to speak with me."

"It was my pleasure," I answer, and this time I mean it. If this is the kind of interview she wants, this is what she'll get. I'm not here to waste any more time with beating around the bush. We'll get straight to the point, and I'll say what I mean, and if Torres doesn't like it, then he can take it up with a lawyer.

As the interviewer leaves, Megan snags my arm and yanks me back into my office.

"What the hell was that?" She asks, voice shrill and distressed. "Are you dead set on ruining your own business?"

I shrug. "People will use the app whether I run my mouth or not. I'm not going to pretend to care about what Torres thinks or feels just because the public expects me to."

Megan looks exasperated. "You know, you make my job a hundred times more difficult than it needs to be."

I smile. "But you love me."

She points at me with a hard finger. "Don't push your luck. And why did I call Thalia today to find out that you basically forced her to quit?"

I raise my eyebrows. "I didn't make Thalia do anything."

"She's afraid, Alec. And you're a damn idiot if you think she's the one who spread the information about you two not being in a couple. Think critically for a moment, please. She loves this job. She wanted to be here. Why would she sabotage her own chances of moving forward in the field?"

I scowl. "Maybe she was tired of being here."

But even as I say it, I know that it's not the truth. Thalia did enjoy being here, and wanted to prove herself every moment of every day. She believed in our goals and had dreams of her own. I even felt sometimes that she believed in me, especially on the night that we came together at last.

Something hits me, hard as a fist to the jaw. It's a realization that terrifies me. Torres saw Thalia walking away that night, alone, dead set on returning home on her own. Maybe he made some guesses, thought that she was leaving me, that we were only pretending for the people in the banquet hall. Maybe he overheard something. Maybe he didn't need Thalia to tell him—maybe he wanted to ruin me any way that he could.

"I need to talk to Torres," I tell Megan, fire in my voice.

"Oh, god," she says with a huff.

# Chapter Sixteen

Thalia

I stare into the mirror in my bedroom, my parents' house buzzing with background noise around me, and smooth my hands over my dress. It's beautiful—fitted and satin, with tiny embellishments of gold and gems that make me look like a work of art. It's stunning, and I feel lovely in it, but I can't fix the vacant expression on my face, the lines seemingly etched into my forehead from all the frowning I've done this past week.

"Thalia? Are you ready?"

My dad's voice carries up the stairs. I tear my eyes from the mirror and scan the room for my shoes, strappy things in a sensible shade of nude.

"Almost! I'll be right down!"

The last thing I want to do is go down those stairs and be whisked away into the world of the political elite. I want to tear this dress off and climb back into bed and try to forget all of it—Megan's words, Alec's cruelty, all the potential I had at Sound Connections.

But instead, I strap the shoes on and hurry down the stairs where my dad is waiting by the door, dressed to the nines in a suit that I'm sure cost thousands. He looks handsome, professional, sure of himself. But those same eyes I've seen all my life are calculating. I can tell that he's looking me over, trying to find something out of place, something that might ruin his chances of making tonight a success.

I know my parents love me. Like I've said before—I'm a lucky girl, never wanting for anything. But there's a difference between guessing that my parents would stand by me if they needed to, and actually feeling their support.

"You're sure that's the right dress for tonight?" My dad asks, his eyes narrowing slightly. I shrug, feeling like I want to cross my arms over myself.

"Mother told me it was a good choice," I said, hating the vulnerability in my voice.

He nods, already mentally moving on, and checks his watch. "Honey! We need to go!"

My mother comes hurrying down the stairs in a beautiful dark blue dress, a fitted thing that nearly reaches her ankles. She looks regal—like she might as well be royalty. My dad's face lights up. My parents might be self-centered and focused on their image over their family, but I can tell that they truly love each other, and that they always have.

I watch them kiss and feel bitterness seep into my heart. Is it so wrong to want something like that for myself? Someone who sees me, all my faults and strengths, and wants me anyway?

Together, we head out to the car where a driver is waiting to whisk us away. Tonight is an event that my dad has been planning for weeks. Despite my recent addition to his team, he put me hard at work at promoting the event and making sure that everything was aligned. It was hard work, I have to admit—the interns he has now are only focused on promoting their own careers, and barely put time into making sure the event itself was ready. But I was lucky enough to watch Megan work before the benefit. I saw exactly what it took to make an event a success, and I implemented everything that I could remember into this night.

We pull up to the venue, and like a slap in the face I realize that it's the exact same one where Alec had his dinner before. The building itself is beautiful, an art-deco masterpiece with intricate details that bloom under the evening light. Emotions come rushing back as I follow my parents up the winding path where I walked with Alec, the two of us heading to his car on the night that we'd let down all our walls and see each other for who we truly are.

Inside, the room has been transformed. It's different from how it was the night of the benefit dinner—the lighting turns the room into a cavern, full of people who are used to spending money without worry.

It's a room crowded with those I need to impress. My dad looks at me over his shoulder, like he wants to drive this point home with me. I smile back, but it's all plastered on.

As we enter the room and someone announces my dad's arrival, people clap for him and conversation explodes throughout the hall. There are people walking around with drinks, people sitting at tables, people laughing and chatting and drinking. I slip away from my parents before they can introduce me to anyone and try to disappear into the crowd.

For a moment, I can almost imagine that I'm back at the benefit with Alec. I try to picture his arm around my waist, his voice in my ear, his laugh low and rough beside me. It's a painful thought, one that I have to erase from my mind before it brings tears to my eyes.

I turn to try and find the bathroom, slowly moving through people who laugh and smile and touch my arm, asking me about my dad and the campaign. I have to keep my fake smile on the whole while as I try to push past them, when suddenly an arm catches my elbow and tugs me back.

"Excuse me—" I start, my mouth falling open in surprise, and my eyes meet Matthew Torres's as he grins at me.

"Sorry about that, I thought I would never catch you. You move quickly, you know."

I pull my arm from his grasp, feeling a chill where he touched me, and try to replace the shock on my face with a smile. My parents would kill me if they ever saw me being rude to someone, especially at an event like this, but Torres is the last person that I ever wanted to see in this moment. I was hoping to have a quiet moment and a good cry in the bathroom, and now I have to pretend to cater to Alec's enemy's interests.

Just looking at him shoots me back to when he found me outside at the last event, questioning me with a sharp glint in his eyes. He had seemed so suspicious of Alec and I. Could it have been Torres that told the tabloids about our relationship? Did someone leak the truth to him?

"Matthew Torres," I say, before I can forget exactly where I am. "It's a pleasure to see you tonight. What are you doing here?"

It's not exactly the kindest question, but I can't stop it from slipping out of my mouth. Torres's face slips a little. A certain hardness outlines his eyes, despite the smiling line of his lips.

"My father is a great fan of yours and wanted to support his endeavor for mayor. Though, I could ask you the same thing. I didn't realize you were working with your father's campaign now. Weren't you working with your boyfriend? Or, no, I remember now—I read about you two splitting up."

Heat rises to my face. "It was time for me to move along."

Torres shakes his head. "Alec is an idiot for letting you go. And all of those awful rumors, that you two were faking the relationship to give Sound Connections some publicity, it's just awful. I can't believe someone would say something like that about the two of you. But Alec has always been an outsider in this field, and he never makes it easier on himself. I'm sorry that you had to get caught up in his mess."

Rage courses through me. Alec might have been an asshole at times, but I'm not going to stand here and listen to someone else talk about him like that, especially not someone like Torres that I know gets a sick pleasure out of someone else's pain.

"Alec works hard," I say, my voice just slightly shaking. "He was a great boss. I just had conflicts in my schedule, and needed to figure out my career path on my own time."

I don't know why I'm defending him, but I can't bear to hear him talk about Alec like that. It feels like a personal attack.

Torres nods slowly, but his smile has morphed into a smirk. "Right, of course. I didn't mean to insult your ex."

The way he says ex feels mocking, like he doesn't believe we were ever together and wants to make that fact known. I give him my nastiest smile—one with teeth and feeling.

"I appreciate your kindness," I say, emphasizing the last word. "I'll be sure to relay your feelings to Alec."

He grins back at me. "I didn't realize you two were still on speaking terms."

We aren't exactly, but I'd never admit that to him. "We decided to remain friends," I say instead, though the lie is sour in my mouth. Torres nods slowly.

"I'm glad to hear it. Well, if you're ever looking for a new position in the same field, Songbird would be lucky to have an employee like yourself. I wouldn't mind having an assistant as beautiful as you," he says with a wink. "Alec doesn't know what he's lost."

I flinch away from his touch as he runs the back of a finger across my arm and try to cover the reaction with a fake cough. "I appreciate that," I say quickly, smiling nervously. "I'll definitely get back to you. If you'll excuse me, I have to help my father with something."

Torres starts to speak but I'm already turning and slipping away from him into the crowd, hurrying into the bathroom where I shut myself inside and try to catch my breath. Panic comes over me as the pieces fall into place. Torres is the only person who would have a reason to try and sabotage Alec. He must have overheard something about the pretend relationship. And while I know he's right in some ways, that we did pretend, that it did begin as a stunt, he didn't know the truth of the matter—that I fell for Alec along the way. That I saw him for who he truly was, unlike everyone else in the world who sees him for his appearance and thinks that he's some delinquent.

I splash some water on my face to calm myself, uncaring if it destroys my makeup. Let them all see me—let them know that I'm not like them.

I have to get out of here. I have to tell Alec my theory, and prove to him that he made the wrong decision when he pointed the blame at me.

# Chapter Seventeen

Alec

It's late at the office, the night already fallen around Malibu. Lights twinkle in the distance past my windows, and I find myself distracted and watching the sunset as I try to wrap up the work still waiting on my desk.

I wonder where Thalia is tonight. She could be anywhere in the city, maybe finding someone new, maybe happier now that she's without me. I was right to push her away, wasn't I? It will save me so much hurt later on.

A knock on my door drags my attention away from the window. "What are you still doing here?" Megan asks as she steps into my office. She's kicked off her heels and is now wearing slippers. I raise my eyebrows at the sight of them and she flips me off. "They're comfortable, okay?"

"You should be home by now," I say. "I'm the only one who needs to be dealing with this disaster."

Megan sighs and sits in one of my office chairs, the one that I've come to think of as hers over the years. "Not true. I created the mess, I clean it up."

"Hey, I agreed with it."

"I forced you."

I roll my eyes with a groan. "No one forces me to do anything. I make my own choices."

"I guess you're right about that one," she says with a laugh. But the grin on her face fades as she looks at me with worried eyes. "I have to tell you something," she adds.

"Go ahead."

"You'll be furious."

I shrug. "I'm always furious."

"I think I know how our secret was leaked. You know Liam?"

I narrow my eyes. Liam is an intern in our marketing department, who I hired because he was great at holding a conversation with anyone he spoke to. He used to work for Songbird before coming to work for us.

"Of course I know Liam," I say impatiently.

"I have reason to believe that he somehow overhead us talking about you and Thalia, and that he gave that information to Torres."

Anger stirs in me. Megan was right—I am instantly furious. It all seems to fall into place—Torres following Thalia out of the venue, asking her strange and uncomfortable questions, his constant attempts to take down Sound Connections and build Songbird up in its stead.

"I'm an idiot," I say, sourly.

"Yeah," Megan responds with a nod, and when I glare at her she laughs. "But so am I! I can't believe we didn't see it. I guess Liam thought he could build a better career if he went back to Songbird."

"I'll kill him," I say with a sneer. Megan sighs.

"Don't kill him. But we can set this right. We can fire Liam, do some more damage control in the press. And you can call Thalia."

My stomach flips. I'm not the type to feel unsure, or out of control, but the thought of being vulnerable with Thalia again is the most terrifying thing that could possibly cross my mind.

"First, I need to speak with Torres," I snap. "Can you find out where he is tonight?"

"Tonight? Are you sure that's a good—"

"Megan," I interrupt. "It needs to be done. I'm not going to let him get away with trying to trash our reputation just to make his shitty company look better."

Megan sighs, but there's a knowing look in her eyes. She's worked with me long enough to know when I'm serious, and right now there's nothing else I'd rather do than chew Torres out and make him regret that he ever fucked with a guy like me.

"I'll see you tomorrow," I say, grabbing my jacket and abandoning my work on my desk. "Text me when you find out his exact location."

"Behave!" She calls after me, but I wave her off in return. I'm not going to make promises that I can't keep.

By the time I'm behind the wheel in my car, I have a text from Megan, stating that Torres attended a gala tonight hosted by...Thalia's dad. However, it's late by now, and I'm guessing the event has already ended. Still—it's worth a shot.

I drive over to the venue. It's the exact same one where we held our own event, and emotion wars inside of me at the memory of spending that night with Thalia...taking her home to my apartment and taking her apart there.

The event seems to be emptied out by the time I park and get out of my car, but it must be my lucky night—I spot Matthew Torres standing near the parking lot on his phone, likely waiting for his driver to bring a car around for him.

"Torres," I call, and I see the surprise in his eyes when he looks up at me. There's a smirk on his face that I want to knock off with a solidly planted fist.

"Lynch," he says with a sneer. "I didn't realize you were invited tonight. I thought you didn't like to involve yourself in politics."

"Cut the shit," I snap. "I've left you to your own devices. I don't understand why you feel the need to involve yourself in my life and business relentlessly."

He raises his eyebrows. "I don't know what you're talking about, Lynch."

But I can see it in his gaze—it's a smarmy knowing expression, one that sends fire racing through my veins. "You know exactly what I'm referring to," I snap. "Your lackey provided you with all the information you needed, didn't he?"

Torres's smile turns into something a little more sinister. "Maybe you should screen the people you hire a little better, don't you think?"

"Maybe you should focus on improving your own business instead of thinking about mine in comparison," I snap. "I don't bother you. I mind my own fucking business and I'm successful because I have an app that people love. Why do you care about what I do?"

"Because you don't deserve the success," Torres says easily, with a smile. "You're what the rest of us despise—good for nothing, overconfident, a waste of time. I don't think you need to be here with the rest of us, so I'm going to do what I can to remove you from the equation. Do you get the picture?"

My fist is moving before I can stop it. I almost hit him, almost knock him back onto his ass, but then my eyes catch a flicker of movement.

It's Thalia, leaving the venue. She looks like a star lit up in the sky. Her hair falls over her shoulders in light waves, and her golden dress hugs her body so beautifully. I stop myself from hitting him and I let my fist drop.

"Alec?" Thalia calls, her voice soft and wounded.

"Call the police," Torres says, his voice full of command. "This animal planned on assaulting me."

"I didn't even touch you," I snarl at him, the anger still burning through me.

Thalia steps up to us. "You need to leave. Both of you."

Torres looks appalled, but he steps back from us. Thalia meets my eyes. She looks so young in that moment, yet so wizened by everything that has happened between us. "Don't do something you'll regret," she says, in a gentle voice. "He's not worth it."

I clench my fist by my side, but I listen to her. She's right. She always is, isn't she? And I never saw that before. But I know better now.

"Fine," I say through clenched teeth, as a car pulls up and Torres shoves past us, getting into the backseat with a slammed door.

We watch him go in silence, the only sound distant crickets chirping in the night and cars rolling past on the pavement.

"Go home, Alec," Thalia says quietly. She won't meet my eyes now. I want to reach for her and pull her into my arms, tell her that I was wrong about everything. But I can't seem to get myself to move.

"Thalia—" I start, but I don't know what to say. How to say it. How to show her that I want her to come back.

"Just head home. It's late."

"But I—" I start to speak, but she turns. "Thalia, wait!"

She stops and looks at me over her shoulder with wounded eyes.

"Come back," I say, under my breath. "We—I need you, back at the office, we need you as a part of our team."

There's a glint clinging to her eyelashes, a shimmer of silver that makes me think that maybe I've cut her deeper than I ever thought possible. She crosses her arms over her chest, and my eyes trace over her, taking in how beautiful she looks in that moment despite the anger coming off her in waves.

"I quit for a reason, Alec. It's not smart for me to work at Sound Connections—you and I both know that to be a fact."

I want to brush her off. I want to say that it's foolish, that all of it is in the past, that it never meant anything. If she wants to forget the night we shared together, I'm okay with that. I just want to be in her orbit. I just want her close to me, stepping into my office again looking radiant and ready to tell me off if needed.

But instead, I say, "You're right." And I try to ignore the way the words dagger into my ribs.

"Go home," she says again.

So I turn, and I walk away.

But that night in my bed, I lie awake all night. When I press my nose to the pillows and toss around in the sheets, I can almost pretend that I smell her—sweet perfume and fruity shampoo, all bright and glowing and warm. I feel like an idiot. I feel like this girl has gotten the best of me, turned my world inside out, made me second guess myself and my goals and exactly what I'm trying to do.

Still, I want her.

I call Megan, despite the blinking red numbers on my clock that tell me it's after one in the morning.

"Alec? What's wrong?" Megan slurs, clearly roused from sleep. "Please don't tell me you killed Matt Torres. I don't have the brain power to make up an alibi for you right now."

"I fucked up, Meg," I say. "And I think you might be my only friend."

I hear her sigh, and then the sound dissolves into laughter. "Okay, idiot. Go to sleep. We'll talk about this in the morning."

I turn over, feeling a little better but still mourning the empty bed that once held Thalia, sweet and slack in her sleep. "Fine." I move to hang up but then I hear Megan's voice on the other end of the phone.

"I'm glad that you're my friend," she says, before she hangs up.

Finally, I can sleep.

# Chapter Eighteen

Thalia

Another day, another overly expensive dinner, where I'm seated across from my parents in a too-tight dress taking tiny sips of my wine.

I wish I could knock the whole glass back and take some of the anxiety off, but I know my dad would give me a disapproving glance and a lecture the whole way home. It's almost worth it, but I can't quite force myself to take the plunge and face the consequences to come.

"My father would love to hear more about that," Matthew Torres says from his position across from my dad, a neat smile on his smug face. His eyes cross over mine and they harden for a moment into something slightly more menacing. Then my dad is answering him with a laugh and Torres tears his eyes from me.

It's been a week since that night, when I saw Torres's true colors and the fight that nearly broke out between him and Alec. A week since I told Alec to go, to leave, to never come back. I regret it every second. I know I did the right thing.

I haven't heard from Megan or Alec—I wonder if they realized that it was likely Torres who leaked our secret, just as I thought. I wonder if he told her that he saw me—if he even still cared, or if he wiped it from his mind.

"Thalia?" My mother asks beside me, and I turn to her in surprise. Her eyebrows are furrowed but there's a pleasant smile still on her lips. "What's wrong?"

"Nothing, Mother," I answer quickly, and I give her an easy smile in response. "Sorry. Just spaced out."

I've had to attend one of these ridiculous dinners nearly every night since the gala my dad held. Each one is exactly the same—everyone vies for my dad's attention and he treats them all to an award winning smile, a wink, a firm handshake. They eat it up. It makes me want to sulk in the bathroom for the remainder of the dinner, hoping that no one will notice I've left.

"You've hardly touched your fish," my mother points out. She's barely eaten any of her own food either, but I know she'd be annoyed if I tried to point that out. I shrug and poke at the piece of salmon, my stomach tossing in protest.

"I'm just not hungry," I say, and my mother turns away instantly, ready to entertain someone else on the other side of the table. I feel invisible in moments like these, only seen when my parents feel like showing me off as the beautiful and quiet daughter they raised me to be. Nights like these are simple, meaningless, empty. I feel like a trophy, in a game that will never be won.

"Songbird," I hear my father say. "Your business is in competition with Sound Connections, correct? That place where you used to work, honey?"

He's looking at me now. In fact, they're all looking at me. I feel my face heat up, my hands numb in my lap.

"Yes, that's the one," I say with a smile that feels like it could slip off my face at any moment.

"That's right," my father says, a thoughtful expression on his face. "Speaking of which—" He starts, but someone's arrival cuts him off.

"Sorry I'm late," Alec Lynch says as he steps into the private room of the restaurant where we're all gathered, appetizers already splayed out across between old money families and businessmen like Alec and Torres both.

My heart does about a hundred summersaults. I blink, over and over, but my mind can't seem to make sense of what I'm seeing. Across from me, Torres does the same, unable to disguise the disgust that crosses his expression. Alec takes an empty seat a few down from Torres, his face pleasant, not quite a smile but a humorous tilt of the lips instead.

"Alec Lynch!" My father says, shocking me completely. "Glad you could make it."

"I'm happy to be here," Alec says with a smirk, though the challenging look in his eyes tells me that he might feel otherwise. His gaze lands on me, and there's heat behind it. At first, I think it's anger. But then his eyes soften at the corners, and I feel a rush to my belly as I recognize that look—desire. Want. Maybe he wants me, just as he did before, just as I still want him. "My apologies again for being late. Someone once told me that it's very rude to be late—I didn't mean to keep you all waiting."

He says this all with his eyes locked on me, and I feel them piercing into me, pinning me in place.

My father laughs. "Don't worry about it, we're happy to have you here. I wanted to gather some of the greatest minds in Malibu for this dinner—I know you all have some fantastic thoughts and opinions, and I believe that I could learn from you amidst this campaign." He glances at me with a slight smile. "I know my Thalia has been active in some of your lives, hard at work. I'm lucky to have her along for the ride."

I give him a weak smile back. Everything feels like too much, all so overwhelming, all so intense. I want to stand up, lean across the table, and press my lips to Alec's. I want to snatch him by the collar and ask why he thinks he can talk to me like he's better than me. And I want him to go home with me, and be held in his arms, and feel my body come to life beneath his.

The table erupts into conversation again. I watch Torres try to refocus my father's attention on him to no avail as Alec starts to chat with the elderly lady seated beside him. She eyes his tattoos warily, but I catch a genuine smile working its way onto her face as they start to talk.

"So," Torres says, as our dessert arrives and a lull lands in the conversation. "How does it feel to be seated across from your ex-boyfriend, Thalia?"

Any remaining chatter dies at his comment. I see Alec turn and fix Torres with his iciest stare. My father clears his throat, and I know that he's about to say something so I cut in instead.

"How does it feel to be second best in every business venture you've ever tried?" I say, with the sweetest smile on my face that I can muster up.

"Thalia," my mother admonishes, aghast.

But Alec is smiling. And that's what matters most to me.

"You're pretty smug for someone who faked your entire relationship just for press," Torres snaps. "How does it feel to know that the whole world knows you as a fraud?"

I laugh. I can't help it—the sound rises out of me instantaneously. "You would know all about pretending, wouldn't you?" I say, the anger building in me, unable to be contained. "You spend every day pretending that your business is actually successful, but everyone knows that your father is the only thing standing between you and bankruptcy."

Torres's face distorts into a mask of calm, but his eyes are burning on me. Alec laughs, actually laughs, out loud.

"I don't know what you're laughing about," Torres grits out. Alec is still grinning as their eyes meet. "You had to force a college kid to be your girlfriend just to get people to download your app."

"He didn't force me to do anything," I say sweetly. "We genuinely like each other. I'm sure that you wouldn't understand."

"Thalia, stop it," my mother whispers angrily.

"So why break up then, if you have nothing to be ashamed about?"

Torres's gaze is a challenge. I won't let him win.

"The rumors that you sold to the press made our relationship impossible."

Torres is enraged. Alec is smiling so wide that I can nearly see each and every one of his teeth, joy radiating in the smile lines around his mouth.

"Don't make accusations that you can't take back," Torres says, his voice low and threatening.

"Speak to her like that again, and I'll destroy you," Alec says, the smile still on his gorgeous face. My heart sings at the sound of his voice. I look at him, and I feel like I'm looking at the sun.

"This ends now," my father says, his voice booming. "I didn't invite all of you for some petty drama. This is a chance for us to connect as people, and I'm not going to sit here and watch all of you argue like children."

Everyone sits in silence for a drawn-out moment. Then, I stand. My parents crane their heads to look at me, shock in their eyes.

"Thalia, please sit down," my mother says.

My father's eyes plead with me, a mix of anger and disappointment.

"I'm going," I say finally. "I can't attend a dinner with a man who is hell-bent on ruining the lives of others." I look at Torres when I say it, my heart in my throat, my pulse thundering in my veins. "I don't want to be a part of this dinner, or this campaign, or the next campaign, or any of it! I want to live on my own terms and I want to work on something I care about, not something that advances the beliefs of people like him."

I push away from the table and ignore the calls of my parents behind me, their voices gradually rising into desperation. I stomp outside into the breezy evening and wrap my arms around myself. The stars overhead are vivid and bright. I don't know where I thought I was going—I rode to the restaurant with my parents, and we're too far for me to walk back home. I guess that I'll be calling a cab.

"Thalia!" I hear behind me. I turn, and there's Alec, jogging after me. Despite our moment across the table, I still feel so uneasy when we're alone, like I'm afraid that he'll accuse me of trying to destroy him again.

"Hi," I say softly when he reaches me. He takes one look at my arms wrapped around me and shrugs out of his jacket before draping it over my shoulders.

"You're incredible," he says, low in his throat.

A smile creeps its way onto my face. "What, that mess in there? That was just a normal Friday night."

He laughs. I love the way it makes his eyes light up at the corners.

"I'm really sorry, Thalia. I know that it wasn't you, and I'm an idiot for even considering that as a possibility. Megan and I found out—"

"That it was Torres, I know," I say quickly. "If I hadn't realized it before, I would have known at this dinner. He's scum, and I know my parents will hate me for arguing with him, but I couldn't bear to sit across from him any longer."

Alec reaches out with a gentle hand and grazes his fingers over my cheek. I lean into the touch. His hand is so warm, the skin rough and soothing all at once.

"Tell me to go home again, and I will," he says. He sounds half-broken, all vulnerability.

"Well, I would," I start, my eyes half-lidded and glancing up at him. "But I kind of need a ride."

He's laughing again, and the sound goes straight to my heart.

"Can I give you a ride to my place?" He asks, one hand pulling me closer to him by my waist. I lean into him, savor the feeling of us pressed together. Every inch where our bodies meet is on fire. I know that I shouldn't go home with him. I know how badly it hurt me before, and this time isn't likely to be much different. But I need it. And denying it from myself will only make me ache worse.

I let him drag me into him. I breathe in the scent of his cologne, made warmer and softer by his skin beneath it.

"Okay," I breathe at last. "Take me home."

# Chapter Nineteen

Alec

There's no hesitation this time, no awkwardness for us to work past. There's no dance to perform where we both pretend that this isn't something we need—I know that Thalia wants me by the way we can't keep our hands off each other. The ride home is agony with her sitting so close to me, just waiting in the passenger seat, needing to be touched. I'm definitely speeding, because we make it back to my house nearly ten minutes before I typically would have made it.

We're kissing before I have the front door shut behind me again. With her mouth against mine, I feel complete, like maybe this moment is what the two of us were made for. Thalia smells intoxicating, with that same perfume I could nearly taste on my sheets now surrounding me again. She feels so small in my arms, so perfectly made to fit against my body, and it's overwhelming to have her pressed against me like this. I want more. I want to make her mine.

"You're amazing," I say into her mouth as we kiss, again and again. I run a hand up her thigh as I press her against the front door. She arches against me and gasps against my cheek.

"Alec," she breathes. "I need you."

"Patience," I murmur against her lips. "I've waited long enough to have you again. I'm not going to rush this."

She laughs but the sound is swallowed into another kiss. She curls her fingers into my hair and I let out a groan at the scrape of her nails against my scalp.

"You're going to tear me apart," I say with a low laugh as she smiles.

"Good," she says. "That's all I want."

She holds tightly around my neck as I scoop her into my arms, my hands settling beneath her thighs. Her dress bunches up around her waist as I carry her to my bedroom, and when I set her down on the bed again I'm overcome by the sight of her, lying there and waiting for me while looking like she's been transformed into a mess.

"Fuck," I breathe. "You're the most beautiful girl I've ever seen."

"I bet you say that to all the interns," she teases, and with a growl I lean in to cover her and nip at her neck. She moans beneath me as I bite a sharp bruise into the base of her throat, a mark that shows that she belongs to me and only me. I love the way my touch makes her move, arching and gasping like she's desperate to feel me all over her.

"You need to watch your mouth," I tease, ghosting my hands over her waist and her hips. She laughs, head tipped back. "I can't believe how bold you've been all night."

"You love it," she gasps, as I kiss down her neck again, scraping gently with my teeth.

She's right. I do love it. I love everything about her, like the way her eyelids are fluttering until they're half shut. I hitch her thighs up around my waist as I kneel over her and I grin when I realize she's wearing thigh high stockings, sheer things with a lacy band that clings to her skin.

"You're wicked," I say roughly. She looks pleased as a cat beneath me as she props herself up on her elbows and beckons me down to kiss her. I feel animalistic, disconnected from myself—this is not how I thought it would be with her, this push and pull of delight, but she's so intoxicating.

"I thought you said I was amazing," she sighs into my mouth, her hand on my jaw sliding along my stubble.

"That too." I press her back into the pillows and kiss her hard, messily. I slip my tongue into her mouth and relish in the velvet feeling of her tongue sliding against mine. It's chaotic and delicious and electric. It's everything I've been thinking about since the last time we were together, and it was worth the wait to have her here like this, opening up for me in my bed.

I nudge her legs apart and she splays herself easily, gasping when my thigh slides between her legs. She arches, lip caught between her teeth. "Jesus, Alec," she says breathlessly.

"Good?" I ask. "You look beautiful like this baby. Now, I just need to get that dress off."

She whimpers and I feel her fingers digging into my back, like she's desperate for something to anchor her in place. Her hips slide against me as she curls a leg around me, trying to pull me closer and hold me against her.

"Not yet," I whisper. "Clothes off first."

I pull back and she sighs at the loss. But I pull her up into a hard kiss again and my hand goes around her back to unzip her dress. I slip the thin straps from her shoulders, the velvety material falling and revealing the delicate lace of her bra and the sinuous lines of her curves. It should be illegal for someone to look so beautiful and spent before I've even had her.

She falls back against the pillows again as I tug her dress all the way down and reveal the matching underwear she has on, along with those devilish thigh highs. I hook a thumb under the elastic band of one and let it snap against her thigh. She gasps a little at the contact, and it brings a smirk to my lips.

"Do you like that?" I ask under my breath, grinning as she nods, her pupils blown wide and the waves of her hair splayed against the pillows. I shrug out of my suit jacket and unbutton my shirt, watching her face all the while. I want her to know that this is all for her, that it's always been for her, that now I realize it always will be and that's how I want it to stay for the rest of time.

I slip my belt free from its loops and leave it to clatter somewhere on the floor. Then my pants follow it, until we're nearly naked together, and I can lean down to press my lips on hers again, feeling the delicious warmth of her skin against mine. There are goosebumps on her arms. I run my fingers over them before I tug her arm up to wrap around my neck.

"Alec," Thalia whispers, her eyes half shut, already wrecked with pleasure just from my touch ghosting over her. Her mouth parts in a gasp as I graze my fingers over her underwear, where I can already feel her wet and wanting. "I need you, please."

"You're going to have to beg harder than that," I say against her cheek, my voice rough and hard with desire.

"Please, Alec, please, I need—" She cuts herself off with a broken moan as I tug her panties down, the intricate lace nearly tearing beneath my grasp. She kicks them off, pressing herself against me, eyelashes as lovely as butterfly wings against her cheeks. I deftly unhook her bra and she shrugs that off too, until she's lying there in nothing but the stockings.

"I think we'll keep these on," I murmur against her ear. "You look too good in them to let them go to waste."

I slide myself between her legs, urging her to lean up against the pillows some more, and I maneuver her legs onto my shoulders.

"I want to taste you," I growl. "Is that what you want?"

"Yes," Thalia sighs, her voice broken.

I press kisses to the inside of her thigh, nipping once in a while, each time getting closer to the wet heat between her legs. She runs a hand through my hair and keeps the other fisted in the sheets. When I finally run my tongue over her clit, she cries out, the sound echoing throughout the bedroom. She dissolves beneath me. I coax gasps and moans and curse words from her lips as she tosses her head back, looking divine in the evening light of my bedroom.

"Alec, wait, I'm going to—ah, hold on—"

I pull back and she tugs me up to kiss her, tasting herself on my tongue. The kiss sends sparks down my body. I haul her thighs up to grind against her waist and she cries out again as my fingers dig into the band of her stockings.

"I want you inside of me," she murmurs. Her cheeks are so pink, the flush moving all the way down her chest to her gorgeous breasts.

The sound of her voice is nearly enough to make me feel feral. I abandon my boxers to the floor and pull her into me, loving the way we fit so perfectly together. I'm so painfully hard, desire clearing everything from my brain besides the sound of her name, repeating over and over in my head until it's the only word I seem to be able to remember.

I reach for the nightstand and grab a condom, rolling it on faster than I thought possible. I feel as if I might die if I don't have Thalia in my arms within the next few moments. Her eyes trail down my body, drinking in the sight of my length hard and ready for her, and she grins so wickedly that I think I could reach ecstasy just from watching the way her mouth forms my name.

With her hands on my back and my mouth on her neck, I slide into her. She moans against my ear, the sound so angelic and sweet. It takes everything in me not to just unfold and fuck into her as hard and fast as we both can bear. Instead, I start to slowly move, my hips snapping into hers, filling her completely with my cock.

We move together like we were made for one another. She's soft and open and desperate beneath me, and everything about her feels incredible and irresistible. We kiss messily, her hands in my hair, mine braced on the bed, her breasts pressing into my chest.

"Alec, please, I'm so close," Thalia gasps, her fingers clutching me tight to her. I'm close, too, my breath coming hard and fast in my chest, my thrusts timed with the sweet sounds she's making. She cries my name again, the sound sharp and desperate. I snap my hips into hers a final time and then she comes with a shout.

"Fuck, Alec!" She cries, and at the sound of my name in her mouth I'm coming too, my body spent and stars blinking at the corners of my eyes.

When it's over, I lower myself against her, feeling our bodies sticky and warm with sweat as they press together. I love every second of it—it feels so right to have her here in my bed again. She strokes a hand over my hair and holds me close to her, exhaling a sound of contentment. I feel her hair against my cheek, her breath ghosting over my ear, her slim waist steady under my hand.

"Wow," I say under my breath. "That was fun."

She shoves at my shoulder and laughs, the sound as light and clear as a bell in the dark. "Shut up," she says, but her voice is so warm that I find myself grinning back at her.

"Only if you stay the night," I murmur.

"There's nowhere else I'd rather be," she whispers back.

# Chapter Twenty

Thalia

I wake to heaven. Alec's arms are wrapped tightly around my waist, his face slack in sleep, shallow breaths exhaling from his nose. The sun streams into the room through the slightly open slats of his blinds. It paints everything a pale gold.

I can't believe that I'm here again, naked in his bed, his touch and his scent all over me. It feels like a dream. It feels like everything that I've ever wanted.

I snuggle closer to him, not ready to give up the sweetness of this moment. I wish that I could fall back asleep and stay this way for the rest of time, just warm and content in his bed, uncaring about the rest of the world. It doesn't matter what the media says, what Torres says, what my parents say. It doesn't matter that this whole thing just started off as a stunt to try to spice up publicity. I know that somewhere along the way, we crossed a line that can never be uncrossed, and now I want Alec to be in my life for as long as he'll have me.

"You're thinking too loudly," he mumbles, a strong tattooed arm hooked around my waist. I relish in the feeling of him everywhere around me, so firm and powerful and tempting. I want to go for another round of the fun we had last night, but I'm in desperate need of a shower and a cup of coffee.

"Go back to sleep," I murmur. "I need to go rinse off and scrounge up something for us to eat."

His grip around my waist tightens. "No way. You're not showering without me."

I laugh and squirm, trying to loosen his hold. "If you're not going to let me up, then you have to get up too. I'm not laying in this bed feeling disgusting."

Alec groans, loosening his grasp just slightly. "Fine, if you insist on torturing me, then we'll get up."

I slide out of the bed and I feel his eyes on me still as I pad around the room, completely naked. I raise my eyebrows at him and he gives me a wolfish grin, one that says he would devour me if he got the chance. I crook a finger at him, beckoning him closer, and we lose ourselves under the hot stream of the shower for longer than I care to admit.

When we're finally cleaned up and close to one another all over again, I steal one of his t-shirts to throw on and start to fiddle with his coffee maker.

"I like the sight of you in my kitchen," he says as he steps into the room, sweatpants hanging low on his hips. I drink him in—the sprawling tattoos all over his chest and abdomen, the damp strands of his dark hair hanging in his eyes. He's so gorgeous, and I can't get over how lucky I truly am.

"I like being in your kitchen," I answer with a little smile. He presses me up against the countertop and kisses me languidly, tongue sliding against mine, his hands hot on my bare thighs.

I break off the kisses to catch his attention. "Hey, I need mugs, and milk, or neither of us will get to enjoy the coffee I just made."

He rolls his eyes but fetches the materials for me, moving comfortably around the kitchen. It feels like a treat to see him so at peace in his own space. Alec sets the mugs down beside me with a soft ceramic clink against the countertop.

"We need to talk about something," he says, his voice pitched low.

I raise my eyebrows. "At least let me have a piece of toast or something first."

He fetches a loaf of bread but his face remains serious. "I mean it. I want to talk to you."

"If this is just an opportunity for you to tell me that all of this was a mistake and you regret it, then you can—"

He cuts me off by cupping my face in his hands, his touch so tender. "Thalia. Please. Just let me talk for a moment. I want to say that I'm sorry. I know I've said it before, but I need to know that you hear me. I'm sorry for the shit that I did and said and I never meant to hurt you, or to blame you for things that were never your fault."

I look up at him, eyes glistening. "It's okay, seriously. I know why you said what you said. I was kind of an asshole too, though you were definitely the bigger dick in the situation."

"I always am," he says with a waggle of his eyebrows, and I pretend to bite the hand holding my face as punishment as he dissolves into laughter.

"Is that all you wanted to talk about? Can I drink my coffee now?"

He kisses me, and it feels like a way to shut me up but I'm not going to complain about it.

"Let me finish," he says against my mouth. He leans back, appraising me with his deep blue eyes. "I want you to come back to Sound Connections."

"Alec," I start. "I don't think that's a smart idea."

"You know that it's what I want, and what Megan wants. You know that it would be good for the company. You're skilled at what you do and you have fantastic ideas. You made the benefit dinner such a huge success, and you taught me how to actually act like a respectable human being for once in my life. Don't you think that matters?"

His eyes are pleading, his mouth turned down at the corners. "You can't tell me that I'm wrong."

I sigh. "So what? People already think that the two of us are a disaster. How do you expect everyone to react when I show up at Sound Connections again like nothing ever happened? Torres will be gunning for me from the day I step into the office again."

"You think I care about him, or any of them?" I watch his face harden, his eyes sure and focused. I shake my head. "Exactly. You know that it doesn't matter to me. I want to keep fundraising with you. I want to build the kids at Malibu High an entire wing for their music classes.

I want them to live a better life because of what you and I will create for them. Wouldn't that be incredible?"

I nod, eyes glistening. "Yeah, it would."

"Good," he says, kissing me hard and nipping my bottom lip when we part. "Then come to work with me on Monday."

"You're sure?"

"One hundred percent sure," he says with a grin.

I smile back at him, his joy contagious. "Fine. I will. But...I need to speak to my parents, if they haven't disowned me by now."

"Why?" Alec asks. "All they want is for you to keep up their reputation. Why do you care what they think of what you do?"

"Because they're my family, and I still love them regardless of the mistakes that they make." I know the words are true as I speak them aloud, resounding. "Because I care about them."

He nods slowly. "Okay, fine, I get it. Take some time to talk to them. But Monday morning, I want to see you in my office. Maybe even a little early, so we could have some time to ourselves." He grins when he speaks, eyes flashing with delight, and I playfully shove his shoulder.

We drink our coffee together, talking quietly and sharing secret glances over our mugs that speak of everything we can't quite say aloud yet. It feels so strange to be here like this with him, always wanting more, always happy to have even this.

We spend the day together, just relaxing in his room and learning things about one another, his arms around me as a movie plays quietly in the background. I feel so lucky to be in this room. I love hearing about his life before Sound Connections—his strained relationship with his parents, the years he spent with next to nothing before the company started to grow, the people who doubted him and the people who supported him along the way. I'm comfortable enough there beside him to nearly drift back into sleep, my arms around his waist, my head on his strong shoulder.

But my phone has been ringing all day, and I can only ignore the fervent buzzing for so long. I pull away from Alec at last and start to gather my things.

"You'll call me if they give you too much shit, right?" He says, the worry in his voice so sweet to hear.

"I will," I promise. "But they're my parents. I know how to handle them, alright?"

He nods, but his face is complicated, like he disagrees. I know he doesn't support my father's visions as mayor, and I can't say that I always do too. But he's still my father. And I still humiliated him at a dinner that he told me was important.

But I'd do it again if it meant standing up for Alec and for myself.

"I'll see you Monday morning," I say, leaning over the bed to give Alec one last kiss before I head out the door.

"You sure you don't want me to give you a ride home?" He asks, eyebrows furrowed.

"I think it would likely only piss them off more to see me arrive home with you," I say with a frown. "I'll take an Uber. Don't worry so much, okay?"

He nods, but I can tell the words aren't quite getting through to him. He sighs and walks me to the door, watching as I leave and waving when the Uber pulls away.

When I finally make it home and step inside, wearing the same dress from last night, the whole place is quiet. I creep carefully into the kitchen, where my parents are sitting across from each other at the dining table.

"Nice of you to show up," my father says, his voice barbed and icy.

"Dad, I'm sorry, I just—"

"I cannot believe your behavior, Thalia," my mother says. Her voice sounds watery and hurt, like she's seconds from crying. "Do you know how much you embarrassed us last night?"

"I'm sorry, okay?" I say, my own voice fragile. I wrap my arms around myself, as if that action will hold me together. "But you both haven't listened to me. You don't understand what I want or who I want or what's important to me. You just choose my life for me and expect me to stand here and watch it all pass by. But I don't want to work in politics, and I don't want to join the campaign. I want to work with Sound Connections and I want to be with Alec."

"I should have never invited that man," my father snaps. "He's a delinquent and he's the cause of everything that went wrong last night. I know you have some twisted idea that he's a good man, but I'm telling you from experience and knowledge that you're making a mistake here, Thalia. You will not see him again, do you understand me?"

I'm trembling—the feeling starts in my fingertips and courses all the way up to my mouth, where anger nearly bursts free from my chest.

"You have no clue what you're talking about," I say, voice nearly shaking. "You think that you can sit there and tell me how to live my life when you don't even know me."

"Thalia," my mother says, her mouth fallen open in horror. "You need to correct your tone, immediately, and apologize to us both."

I shake my head and cross my arms over my chest. "It's always been about your money and your reputation, with both of you. Even when I was growing up. You've never stopped to ask me if I wanted a different life, or if I had dreams beyond the things you forced me into. What I believed in didn't matter to you and it still doesn't. Sometimes, I think that it never will."

"Now you're just being ridiculous," my mother snaps. "We gave you everything you could have ever wanted. You've had a beautiful life."

"I'm grateful for what you've provided for me. But I don't want to sit here and wait while you tug me along into whatever predestined venture you have planned for me. I want you to know me. I want you to want to know me. I want to feel like we connect because you're proud of me, not because I'm acting like the daughter you always wanted."

There are tears blooming at the corners of my eyes, and my breath hitches in my throat.

"Go to your room," my father says, his voice ice cold. He won't look at me.

"Actually, I have somewhere else to be."

I storm out of the house before either of them can stop me. Now that I've said my piece, there's nothing else that can be done. I just have to hope that they'll ruminate on their love for me, if there's anything left.

I hurry down the sidewalk and start walking in a random direction. I don't care where I end up, as long as it's far from the house and my family.

The sun is fading around me by the time my feet carry me to their unknown destination—the beach, just a few blocks from our house. I step onto the sand and find a spot near the surf where I sit down, taking in the calling gulls and the crashing echo of the waves. It's peaceful here, and I can hear my thoughts for the first time in what feels like ages.

It seems simple, sitting here, waiting for the tide to come in and the moon to rise from behind the clouds. There was never any other answer—I want to work with Alec, and I want to be at Sound Connections, and I want to live the life that I was so close to having. I want to graduate and be my own person, and I want to build a future with Alec that I can be proud of.

I fish my cell phone out of my bag and ring Alec's number. He picks up in seconds, sounding breathless on the other end of the line.

"Everything okay?" He asks, sounding concerned.

No, I want to say, everything is a disaster, but my family is my own issue to handle. I want to share the excitement with him, not the dread.

"I'll come and work with you," I say. "I'll come back to Sound Connections."

Alec lets out a light breath that dissolves into a happy laugh. "That's what I was hoping you'd say."

# Chapter Twenty-One

Alec

"I do have my demands, if we're going to make this work," Thalia says with a sly smirk on her lips as we sit down in my office on Monday morning.

I lean back in the chair behind my desk, tapping my fingers against the arm of the chair. I raise my eyebrows at her. She looks so beautiful that it's nearly impossible to keep my hands off her—her hair is tucked behind her ears, her lips painted in a sinful shade of red, and the dress she's wearing hugs every dip and curve of her body in beautiful ripples of satiny fabric. She crosses her legs at the knee and challenges me with her gaze.

"Demands, huh?" I say, my voice rough around the edges. It takes everything in me not to reach for her and tug her into my lap. I want to bend her over this desk and claim her for my own, let everyone hear how well we belong together. But I simply fold my hands over my chest instead—maybe, after everyone leaves this evening, the office will be our place to defile. "Tell me what you need, baby."

I say the words mostly just to make her flush, and I can tell that I'm successful when her ears tinge red.

"I don't want to have the job of an intern," she says, voice steady despite the twinkle in her eyes. "I know that I'm not technically one, but I'm still doing intern tasks, and I want to be in the thick of the fundraising. I want to plan events and watch the funds we raise go directly to causes I believe in and feel strongly about. I want to help you support the places that you know need assistance to grow and change."

I nod along with her words. I can't tear my eyes from her—passion ignites there, a real fire that blooms when she mentions the causes that she believes in.

"That can be arranged," I say evenly. "So what do you want? A raise? An office of your own?"

Her gaze sparkles. "I mean, some bonuses like those couldn't hurt."

I grin. "Okay, done. That's easy. What else?"

She leans forward in her seat, her lips parting with excitement. Her hands start to wave as she talks, like she can't contain the thrill that's bursting forward from her chest. "I want to start by hosting an event that the people we're benefiting can actually come to. I'm sick of benefits where every person invited is a well-off and haughty and ready to mingle with the elite. If we're supporting the high schoolers in Malibu, I want them to come and make an impression and be a part of the growth we're creating. Maybe that means they're playing music and showing the donors what kind of talent they have. Maybe they're just having a fun night with good food. No matter what it is, I want them to feel involved, not like they're just a charity case."

I can't help it—a bright smile spreads across my face. I wonder what it would have been like for me to grow up as an underprivileged kid with a role model like Thalia to look up to. I would have been cautious of her at first, knowing her background and the life she's lived up to now. But to hear her talk about the causes she believes in and the equality she wants to promote fills me with a contagious passion.

"You're something else," I say with a grin, a challenge in my eyes as my gaze meets hers.

Thalia shrugs. "I try," she says slyly.

"Fine," I respond, sitting up and dragging my chair closer to my desk. "These are good points. They're really good, in fact. I think they're all possible, too, if you're willing to work for them."

"Always," Thalia says with a smile. "And I know the perfect place to start."

With that, we kick off the plans for our next big event. Thalia has a grand vision for a garden party downtown at the Botanical Gardens where we took our photos together. There, we'll invite the same elite donors that have kept up with Sound Connections and supported the work that we create. The party will also invite all the local kids at

Malibu High School, and we'll have a guitar performance using the new instruments we provided after the last fundraiser.

We pull Megan into the set up as well—we'll need caterers, the venue, drivers, décor. This is Megan's specialty, and she seems more than thrilled to work on a project like this—especially now that Thalia is back in business.

"I'm so glad you're back," Megan says as we gather in the conference room and start making notes about everything that needs to be done to make the event possible. "Never leave me alone with Alec again. He was insufferable while you were gone."

"Excuse me," I say, flipping Megan off as she rolls her eyes at me. "You're acting like I won't fire you tomorrow."

Megan snorts out a laugh. "Yeah, good luck with that one."

"Focus," Thalia says, snapping her fingers at her. "We need this project on track."

Megan raises her eyebrows at me. "See, aren't you glad she's back?"

We spend the rest of the week bringing plans together and making everything fall into place. There's a lot to be considered to make an event successful, and it's never been my strong suit. But having Thalia here is helpful and let's me work with her while letting some of the work slide off my plate—instead I get to focus on the app itself again, making sure that our servers are running smoothly and that the careful publicity Megan put into place after our stunt is going over well.

By the end of the week, Thalia stops by my office in a rush, a pleased smile on her face. Being back at this job suits her so well—now that she has her own office, she always looks like she's in her element, thriving on the work that she's creating.

"I have an idea," she says with a smile. "Want to go on an adventure with me?"

"Why?" I ask, looking up from my screen. "Where are we going?"

"Don't ask questions, dummy—I just have an idea. Trust me."

I'm not one to be suspicious of her ideas after knowing how well they can turn out—so I nod, and I let her drag me across Malibu as the day winds to an end.

She drives us down the winding roads late in the afternoon. The sun fades in golden rays as she takes hard turns and speeds a little too fast for my taste, though she sputters when I point out her poor driving. Finally, we park at a community center.

"What are we doing here?" I ask, questioning her with a heavy gaze.

I know that Thalia doesn't know much about my past besides the few details I've shared with her, but it seems that she understands more than I've shared just out of instinct. I used to spend so many nights at this community center when both of my parents had to work late—it's where I first connected with some other kids who showed me bands that they liked, and I got to start discovering music that was special to me.

It feels like fate that we're here together. She looks at me with a sheepish smile as she leans against the steering wheel. "Ready to talk to some teens?" She asks, smile curling up at the corners of her lips.

"Talk to teens? What am I, a motivational speaker?" I ask, tone teasing, but her words make me feel a little out of control. Does she expect me to be a good example for these kids? Even knowing that I'm probably the worst possible person she could choose to speak to them?

"Come on," she says. Then she leans across the center console of the car and kisses me, hard, one hand cupping my cheek. "I want to show you off to everyone as the incredible man that I know you are."

I smile against her lips. It's crazy how light she makes me feel, like years of anger have worn away and left me in their wake.

"Fine," I say, and she claps with delight.

We walk into the community center together. The evening is beautiful and bright. Inside the community center, I can hear children's voices rising and falling, the squeak of sneakers, peals of laughter. A kind woman sitting behind a desk at the front leads us back to a cafeteria-esque room where groups of young kids are hanging out and talking. Everything is too familiar and entirely foreign all at once. Being in these halls makes me feel like a kid again, in a way that makes my chest ache.

"Hey everyone," the secretary says. The kids look to her with trust—they know this woman, have spent years coming to this very place. They clearly feel comfortable with her. I hope that's a good sign for us. "I have two friends here who want a few minutes of your time to talk about your opinions."

Everyone turns to face us. I feel the weight of their gazes—we must look strange up here, these two people invading their space. Thalia done up in her work dress and high heels, me with my dark shirt and exposed layers of tattoos.

"Hey guys," Thalia says warmly, in that tone of voice that manages to ease all the tension I have stored up in the arms I cross over my chest. I don't know how she does it, but the kids seem more comfortable with her there, smiling in front of them. "I'm Thalia, and this is Alec. We're here to talk to you about music. Does anyone like to listen to music?"

Nearly every hand in the room goes up. They're rapt, paying attention to her and nodding along to their words.

"I totally agree," she says with a grin. "What about playing music? Do any of you play an instrument?"

A few hands go up around the room, but the responses are scattered. Thalia looks at me with a smile. "Well, how many of you would like to learn?" She asks them, but her eyes still drag over me. More hands shoot up now, the enthusiasm back in the room.

Thalia takes a seat at a table in the center of the room and encourages everyone to gather around. She pats the seat next to her and I join her, feeling entirely out of my element. The kids gather around us. This close, I can tell that they're a range of ages—teens and middle schoolers and young kids just starting out in the world are all over, tired expressions in their eyes but laughter in their mouths.

"I like your tattoos," a kid says to me as he sits across from me. Under the table, Thalia pats my knee, like she's encouraging me to speak up. This isn't my thing—I don't like to speak in public, and I definitely don't know how to talk to these kids. But I clear my throat and give the kid an easy smile.

"Thanks, man," I say. "It's from a song—"

"I recognize the lyrics," the kid interrupts quickly. He smiles. "That band made me want to learn how to play guitar."

"Do you go to Malibu High?" I ask.

"Yeah, most of us do, if we're not at Malibu Middle School still."

I nod. "Good. I went there too. And I know that it's not the best place on earth, but you'll have opportunities there, and it's worth spending time trying to build something that you can be proud of. You get me?" A few kids nod along with my words. "That's why we're here. Thalia and I have a company called Sound Connections. You all probably aren't old enough to join the app, and I hope that you're focusing on schoolwork before dating—" quiet snickers echo around the room, and I can't help but smirk— "but we know the power of music and the connections it can open up around the world for people, no matter where you're from. So we're here to hear from you guys—what are you interested in? What kind of music do you want to play? If you could do anything—see any concert, have any instrument—what would you want?"

Slowly, one by one, they start to open up to us. They tell us about the bands they love and the concerts they want to see. They talk about rapping and songwriting and staying afterschool to practice because there aren't enough instruments for them to take them home.

And by the end of the evening, we all feel comfortable with each other, and a few of the kids even ask me for my email for future internship opportunities. They're great kids, and it makes me happy to see them so enthusiastic about the chances we're trying to build for them. Thalia tells them about the event we're planning, and invites them all to A Night of Music in the Malibu Botanical Gardens.

"You did so well," Thalia whispers against my ear as we head out to her car. I snatch her keys from her hand and lean in to give her a hard kiss.

"It's all thanks to you," I say with a grin, laughing at the betrayed look that comes into her eyes. "Now, let me drive us home."

"Home?" She asks, raising an eyebrow.

"I mean, my home, if you'll stay for the night."

She grins, but there's something sad in her eyes. "Of course. It's not like I want to go home right now anyway."

There's something unspoken there—but I won't push her. If she wants to talk about it, she'll open up to me. Instead, I drive us home, her hand on my forearm and a dreamy look in her eyes.

That night, we don't sleep very much. Instead, I lose myself in the beautiful creature that she is.

# Chapter Twenty-Two

Thalia

The next two weeks pass by in a fevered flash. Every waking hour is packed with another task that needs to be done—class, homework, actual work, event planning—and it's all almost too overwhelming. But being in the office with the people I've come to really enjoy spending time with makes it all a revolutionary time. I'm finally satisfied with the world that I'm building for myself, even if I've barely spoken to my parents in the past few weeks.

But now the garden party is coming up. We've planned an auction, where we'll have some luxurious items and activities up for grabs, along with food catered by local restaurants all around Malibu. There will also be performances by the high school students, with music that anyone could enjoy. It will be a success. It has to be a success.

I take Alec to get fitted for another suit—he's much more cooperative this time, willing to let me pick and prod and coax him into something sleek. We settle on a deep green suit so dark that it's almost black. He looks devilishly handsome in it, and it nearly steals my breath out of my chest to see him standing in that fitting room.

This time, though, it's not just Alec who needs to shop around for something to wear. Megan gives me the company card and tells me to go wild.

"Trust me. That man owes you more than just a beautiful dress," she hints with a waggle of her eyebrows in Alec's direction one morning. "Pick out something you love. Have fun. This auction is going to be a direct result of all the hard work you've put into it these past few weeks, and I think it's worth treating yourself in the meantime."

I can't help it—I pull Megan into a tight hug. She makes a little oof sound but hugs me back, hard.

"I can tell why you mean so much to Alec," I say, my voice dangerously close to wobbling. "I'm really glad I get to work with you again, Megan."

"Oh, don't be such a sap," she says, but she's grinning, the smile so wide it nearly splits her face in half.

I take her up on her recommendation and drag Alec around to a few designer boutiques. While my parents have always been well off and have provided me with wonderful things, I constantly felt guilty when any amount of money was spent on me. It takes me a while to break free from that mindset as Alec and I walk through some of the most beautiful arrangements of evening dresses I've ever seen, but the way his eyes go dark and hungry when he watches me slip into a silky sage green dress is enough to convince me to swipe the card.

We go to dinner after our shopping trip. The weather has finally warmed up again, summer creeping across Malibu, evident in the flowy dresses and sandals that have emerged among the people around us. The breeze tousles my hair as Alec holds my hand, leading me into the restaurant. I hear a few camera shutter clicks behind us—paparazzi, trying to keep up with whatever development has clearly gone down in our relationship. I'm not going to explain it for them, so let them struggle to figure out what's going on.

"I'm worried," I say as we sit down and a waiter uncorks a bottle of wine for us. Alec doesn't answer right away, just raises his glass to clink it against mine and then sips thoughtfully. I can't get over how beautiful he looks, how lucky I am to sit across from him knowing that he's mine. That tonight, he'll take me home with him and make me forget every heavy thought that plagues my mind.

"What's there to be worried about? Don't stress so much, sweetheart. Everything is going to be totally fine." His voice is reassuring, but his eyebrows narrow when he sees that his words clearly aren't working on me. "Tell me about what's bothering you. Maybe I can help."

My voice feels weak in my throat. I really shouldn't be stressed—the event is all set up, totally ready to go, with everything falling into its perfect place. But I can't help the panic that rises in my chest, demanding to be felt.

"There are just so many different pieces that need to be perfect. The food, the music, the auction, the performances—there are too many opportunities for everything to fall apart. And...I invited my parents."

Alec's eyebrows raise. "You did?"

I haven't told him the full extent of the argument I had with my parents—it feels too personal, too mine. While I trust him completely, part of me still wants to hold onto that fight for myself to work through on my own time, with no one else's influence.

"I did," I say, swallowing hard around another sip of wine. "But it will be fine, right? What could they possibly do at an event full of people?"

My father would never put his reputation at stake. He would show up, pretend to have a wonderful time even if he wasn't actually feeling that way. He'd show his appreciation for the students and the music they were playing with a bright smile on his face. But afterwards...I just can't see him or my mother forgiving me for the things that I said, even if they were the truth. And that's what scares me—I thought I would have my parents in my life forever. And now it's up to them to make that decision.

"It's going to be perfect," Alec promises. "If they decide to say anything out of pocket, I'll be there to steer you away from it. As long as you promise to keep me in check, too."

He smiles, teasingly, and I can't help but grin back. His foot brushes mine under the table. I can't believe that this is where I feel safest—with this man who used to terrify me, with his icy eyes and rippling tattoos and pure muscled strength. But now, he's everything that feels like home to me. It feels like we've known each other all our lives, while we're simultaneously learning something new about each other every single day.

"We still have two weeks before the event," Alec says, his tone low and soothing. "Maybe they'll come around in the meantime. I know you mentioned that you all haven't been talking to each other much, but give them time. If your father is anything like me, it can be ridiculously easy to hold a grudge."

I roll my eyes, but a smile plays at my lips. "You're right. Okay. Everything will be fine."

"I'm always right," he promises, a devilish glint in his eyes. "Now, how about we finish up this meal, and I take you home and show you just how right for you I can be?"

Heat flushes all the way down my body. I take a long sip from my wine glass, holding his eyes over the rim. "I'd like that," I say, voice husky with desire.

And that night he does just that—proving that we were made to fit together, that we'd always fit together, his mouth on mine and his hands all over my body.

I never thought I could love someone like I love Alec. And I do love him—I've known that to be true since the night I saw him after my father's event, his face so forlorn and desperate in the dark. I looked at him and I knew that this was the man who held my heart. It's a terrifying thought, to think that there's someone in the world who holds such a tender part of you, but it's undeniable. I love Alec Lynch. And I know that he loves me when he holds me through the night, whispering my name against my ear, his hands painting works of art across my back in light, sweet touches.

He says it a few nights before the event. In his bed, he holds me so close to him that I feel I could almost melt into him, become one with his skin.

"I love you, Thalia," he says quietly, his breath ghosting over the top of my head. "I want you to know that. Even when everything else feels like it's falling apart, you have me, and I love you, and we're never going to be apart again."

I look up at him. The evening light ignites his face into a thousand shades of gold. "Promise?" I ask him, feeling tears spring to the corners of my eyes.

"I promise," he says, and he punctuates the statement with a warm kiss on my lips. Then his eyebrows scrunch up as he smirks. "Now say it back, asshole."

I dissolve into laughter as he squeezes me close to him, and it takes me a few tries to get the words out. "I—I love you too, Alec. You know that."

"I do," he says, nodding sagely. "But I wanted to hear you say it."

Then, finally, it's the night of the garden party and the auction. I get dressed at Alec's place, him in his suit, me in my dress, the two of us suiting one another so well. He tells me I look beautiful, and I let his words sink into me, anchoring me, allowing me to feel the truth in them. He thinks I look beautiful. Maybe I do look beautiful. Maybe today is the beginning of the rest of my life.

A driver picks us up and takes us over to the venue an hour early, where Megan is already waiting. The whole place is done up in stunning twinkling lights. There are fountains spouting water and flowers blooming in every direction, colorful and warm with the scents of summer. People mill around—there are caterers preparing trays of hors d'oeurves and staff setting up instruments on different stands around a small stage, illuminated with warm lights and draped in fine cloth. The whole thing looks like a scene in a play, fairy-like and bright. The sight of it all ignites pride in my heart. I can't believe that we made this a reality.

"Ready?" Alec asks me, and I nod, looking up at him with adoration in my eyes. I feel so blessed to be standing here beside this man.

"There you two are," Megan says, a wicked grin on her face. She looks gorgeous in a pale blue pantsuit. Her hair is slicked back. Her entire look is chic and impressive, every inch the kind of businesswoman we know her to be. "Isn't this place gorgeous? Everyone really transformed it within the past few hours." She tilts her head back, taking in the lights and décor. Then her eyes land on me, twinkling. "Ready, Thalia?"

"Ready," I confirm, smiling back.

People start to arrive soon after. Alec and I welcome many of the kids we met at the community center—they're done up in clothes that Alec provided, crisp button downs and slacks and dark dresses. I can see the excitement in their faces, and it builds up my own joy.

The event fills out with a huge range of people. The kids line up on stage and play a guitar number that has the whole crowd clapping along. Alec greets people with a smile on his face that I feel we would have never seen just a few months ago. He seems transformed into someone who thrives on this energy, who has fun at events instead of resenting them.

"Thalia," a voice says behind me, and I turn to find my father there.

"Dad," I say, my voice cracking around the word just slightly. I clear my throat and smile at him. "I'm glad you could make it."

He's smiling too, but it doesn't quite reach his eyes. There's a sadness there that feels untouchable. "This is beautiful, honey. You did a great job."

His words flare to life in my chest, sweet as honey and light as air. My mother steps up beside him and pulls me into a hug. It's the touch I've been waiting for these past few weeks, and it nearly breaks me down into tears.

"We're proud of you, honey," she says against my ear. I squeeze my eyes shut. "I know there's a lot we need to talk about, but I want things to be okay between us again. Can we try to forget that whole mess?"

I nod against her shoulder, warm in her embrace. "I don't want to forget it," I say quietly. "But I want to move past it. And I want to do that with both of you in my life, standing by my side, and supporting me in the decisions that I make."

She rubs a hand across my back and I hold her as tightly as I can until she finally pulls away. Then my father pulls me into his arms too. Now I really have to hide my face, hoping the tears that slip free don't ruin my makeup.

"If you're happy, then I can be happy," he says. "It's clear that you're building a successful life for yourself, and I want to be there to watch it grow."

"I want you there too, Dad," I say, and he hugs me even tighter. When they finally pull away from me, I wave them off.

"Go, have fun, eat something and schmooze. I know you're dying to." My father grins at my words and gives me a playful little salute.

"You know me well. We'll be around, especially when the auction starts. I'm excited to see these performances you've promised."

They slip into the crowd and Alec leans in to kiss me softly. "Everything alright?" He asks, voice pitched low.

"Everything is just fine," I promise, and I smile up at him with meaning.

# Chapter Twenty-Three

Alec

The auction is finally beginning. The gardens are packed with people milling around. I even spot Mr. Johnston with some of his students as they wrap up an orchestra performance of a pop song. The kids sound great. I make a mental note to plan for an entire revamp of their string instruments, along with music stands for each and every kid.

Megan leads Thalia and I over to the stage. I don't know why I agreed to be a speaker at this event, but something about that pleading look in Thalia's eyes made it so impossible for me to say anything other than yes. She's shining now, gorgeous in her curve-hugging dress. The lights play off the tints of blonde in her hair and paint her in a million bright shades. She takes my hand, and it's all the encouragement I need to step onto the stage and face the crowd of people that I used to think hated my guts just for my past and the way that I looked.

Now their faces are shining back at me. Now everyone is rapt with attention, eagerly waiting for what I have to say.

"Welcome everyone," I say, my voice clear and sure. I don't know where this control comes from; maybe it's buoyed by the presence of Thalia at my side. "The past few months have been a wild ride in my world. This event is meant to celebrate the wins along the way—I hope that you're excited to share in this joy with Thalia and I."

The crowd cheers, a great wave of applause echoing across the garden.

"I won't beat around the bush. I know you all came to participate in our auction and to hear these talented kids play. Tonight, we're raising money for a cause that's near and dear to me," I say, meeting Mr. Johnston's eyes across the garden. He's smiling with pride and joy in his eyes.

"We're funding a brand-new wing at Malibu High School, where music studies will be the primary focus. Malibu High will now have the opportunity to provide students with a conservatory level education. The funds we raise tonight will go toward the new building, instruments, events, and teacher pay, to make sure that our educators have the resources they need to get these kids where they deserve to go."

The crowd cheers again, a raucous cry that brings a grin to my face. "With that said, let's get to the actual auction, okay?"

Thalia helps me show off each item. There's a guitar signed by all the kids along with instruments donated by musicians all across California. There are collectible items, rare items, memorabilia that haven't seen the light of day in years. There are music classes and performance tickets ranging from ballet to concerts. We raise thousands by the fourth item up for auction, and I watch Thalia's face light up each time she gets to shake someone's hand and thank them for their donation.

"This is incredible," she says to me as we move down the list of items. "I can't believe it's going so well."

I memorize the look on her face—absolute joy, untouched by fear or hesitation. Her brown eyes are warm as honey. Her lips are pink and kissable, just waiting to be touched. She looks incredible, and I know in that moment, I want her to be mine forever.

We wrap up the last item as we break the $300,000 line. Thalia throws her hands up in the air as it sells—a collection of guitars that were used on tour with the Beatles are now in the hands of a very happy music fanatic.

"We have one more thing," I say into the microphone as Thalia hugs the person collecting their bid. She turns to face me, surprise in her eyes. "Megan, if you could help me out here?"

Megan jogs up the stairs to the stage and fishes something out of her pocket, passing it over to me. She gives me a wink that says everything as I thank her.

I turn to Thalia. "I thought that was the last item?" She asks, eyebrows raised in question.

That's when I sink to one knee and show her the box that Megan has handed me.

It feels like time freezes around us, all sounds disappearing. It's just me and Thalia there in that moment, suspended, watching each other with sparkling eyes and wide smiles. I want this moment to last forever. I want to shut my eyes and think of her like this, looking down at me, waiting for me to speak.

Thalia is stunned, her mouth dropped open, her hands pressed over her heart. Her eyes are rimmed in silver before I can even open my mouth.

"Thalia Weaver," I say, my voice steady. The crowd is roaring around us. "I know we haven't known each other long. But you have changed my life. I can't imagine a single moment without you in it, and I want to spend the rest of my days with you by my side. Would you do me the honor of being my wife?"

A single tear rolls down her cheek as she breaks into a blinding smile. "Of course I will," she says, and she laughs as I slide the diamond onto her finger. It fits so perfectly, made just for her. I can't hear anything but the pounding of her heart as I scoop her into my arms and the crowd screams their approval. She kisses me with all the passion and force I've come to associate with her. She tastes sweet as sugar, her lips parting under mine, and I smile into our kiss. I'm the luckiest man on earth.

"Thanks everyone for joining us in this special moment," I say into the microphone. "Now, please enjoy the Malibu High marching band—we'll see them at Nationals next year, I can guarantee it."

I lead Thalia off the stage as the music starts up behind us. She's giddy and breathless, her smile almost too bright to look directly at it.

I feel like I've changed the trajectory of my life in the last few months. Before Thalia, everything felt stagnant—I hated to be around other people, only felt comfortable behind my desk and with loud music echoing around the office. I spent years trying to prove to everyone that I'm the kind of person worthy of respect and found so many of them distrusting in the process. I was exhausted by trying to show rich people that my past didn't define me—that the years of screwing around with my friends and getting in trouble were just a way for me to try to understand myself in the process.

Now Thalia looks at me like she can see all of that, and still doesn't care. She loves me for who I am, regardless of the uncomfortable moments we've been through. She's here, and she's wearing my ring on her finger, and I'm never letting her go.

"I can't believe you," she says, kissing me again and again and then sneaking glances at the ring on her left hand when she pulls away from me. "How did you hide this from me?"

"I have my ways," I say low in my throat. I tap her chin lightly with my finger and kiss her languidly again. I can feel the same electricity that always sparks through me when I touch her. It's an amplified feeling that lights me on fire.

Then, someone clears their throat near us—I turn and my eyes land on Matthew Torres. I'm surprised that I don't try to knock him out as soon as our gazes meet, but I manage to hold myself back.

"What are you doing here?" I snap, feeling the moment crash hard in my chest.

He holds up his hands in defense. "I'm not here to destroy your moment, I promise. I'm here to share my best wishes for your long and happy future together."

His eyes travel over the two of us. "I don't claim to understand how your relationship began, but I'm happy for you. And I'm...I'm sorry for what unfolded between all of us. It was wrong of me to try to sabotage what is definitely a connection between the two of you. It's clear that you love each other and that you're trying to do good for the community. I'm not going to stand in the way of that."

I admit—it feels good to hear him say that, even if I don't totally believe what he's saying.

"Thank you," Thalia says at last, when I can't find the right words to respond with. Torres smiles. For the first time, it doesn't look like it's full of venom. "I'm sorry for calling you out at a dinner full of people."

Torres scoffs. "I suppose I was asking for it," he says with a grimace. But there's still a sly glint to his eyes, one that tells me not to trust him. I've spent years battling with this man, and he's not going to slip out of that so easily. "Well, I'll see you two around—I'm sure we'll be spending plenty of time together as the campaign continues, and Songbird intersects with Sound Connections."

He extends his hand for me to shake. I eye it suspiciously, but Thalia nudges my side, so I finally take it and give it a shake. His grasp is firm—it feels like a challenge. But this time, it's not malicious. It's just the two of us pitted against each other like we've always been, each trying to prove that our business is worth what we say it is.

Torres gives us both a nod and slips back into the crowd. I slide my arm around Thalia's waist and tug her into me, safe and comfortable at my side.

"Hey you two!" Another voice calls, and this time it's Megan. She hurries over to us, heels clicking on the stone path, and yanks us into a big hug.

"Hungry?" I ask Thalia, and she nods, her eyes wide as she takes in the packed garden. It seems that everyone is having fun—music plays from the stage where the band is alive with arrangements of a pop song, the whole crowd clapping along. We try to disappear into the thick of it and snatch a few appetizers off a table, but we get caught again, this time by...Thalia's father.

I know I probably should have asked for her parents' permission before proposing. But after seeing the way they treated her, like she was misbehaving just by existing, I didn't feel that they deserved the courtesy.

Now her father is watching me like a hawk, his eyes trained and sharp. "Congratulations," he says, and his tone is warmer than I expected. He holds a hand out to shake, just like Torres did, and after a beat I take it. His grasp is even harder than Torres but I hold his gaze and let him know that he's not in charge here—we're equals, and while we both might love Thalia, I'm here to protect her too.

"Thank you, sir," I say, tone even. "Your daughter is very special to me."

I watch the words register with him. I know that he's suspicious of me, that he doesn't want to let her go. He raised her with such a specific idea for her future and now he has to struggle to put the pieces back together, with everything changing in front of him. I know that it's difficult for him to wrap his mind around, but Thalia makes her own decisions, and I'll stand by her and defend the choices she puts into place until the end of time.

"She's a wonderful girl," he says, sounding wistful, and his eyes land on Thalia. She's smiling back at him. There's a wounded look to her gaze, but joy is there too, reflected in the softness in her face.

Her mother steps up beside them and stretches her arms out for Thalia. They pull each other into a hug. "I'm so happy for you baby," her mother says, and I can hear the tears in their voices. "I'm sorry for everything that happened. You know how sorry I am. I'm just glad to see you two so happy."

"I can trust you to take care of her, can't I?" Her father asks me. I can see the quiet air he carries with me. He's been defeated in some way, lost the future he had projected onto Thalia, and now he's coming to terms with the life that she's choosing. It's a hard adjustment, I can imagine, but it's one that he'll have to make to keep Thalia in his life.

"Dad," Thalia says with a scolding tone. "Alec is incredible. No one has ever taken care of me better. Besides, sometimes I need to take care of him too," she adds with a waggle of her eyebrows. I raise my own back at her, a challenge.

"We'll all have to have a dinner together," her mother says, clapping her hands with finality. "I want to get to know you better, Alec. You seem like a truly wonderful man, if you were able to capture my girl's heart so quickly."

I look at Thalia. She carries the sun in her face, all shining light, shades of flickering gold. She's the most beautiful girl I've ever seen, and my heart nearly skips a beat when her lips stretch into a smile.

"I'm the lucky one here," I say softly. "Your daughter is a gift to this world."

Her mother's eyes look misty when they meet mine. Thalia squeezes her hand.

"Okay, enough of the sappy talk," Thalia cuts in. "I'm starving—can we get some food?"

Her father laughs and they follow us over to the spread of appetizers as we pick at the options and fall into easy conversation. Her parents still seem a bit suspicious of me, but with Thalia there smiling so wide and happily looking up at me between bites, they settle into the moment. I think that, with time, I'll be able to win them over.

Overall, I think, looking at Thalia with devotion in my eyes, the night was an absolute success.

# Chapter Twenty-Four

Thalia

After the success of our auction and the surprise proposal, Alec and I go back to work as fiancés, ready to take on the world.

It feels so special to finally have some semblance of approval from my parents. We visit their home for dinner almost every week, and I think they're starting to really like Alec. They can see that he's smart, funny, and even charming now that I've had the opportunity to school him on his talking skills a bit. And now that I'm basically living at Alec's place, it's nice to have a chance to see them. My father's campaign is ramping up and it seems like he'll be the new mayor of Malibu pretty soon. While it feels intimidating to think of him that way, he's still just my father, and I'm still just Thalia to him. But we're different now. He respects the work that I'm doing and values the changes that I'm making in the community.

That's worth all the struggling, isn't it? A moment of change. A breath of fresh air. I feel like we're both growing and changing, building a different life for ourselves, one where we coexist with our own standards and dreams.

As we adjust to our life together, I finally graduate college. Alec gives me a standing ovation at the ceremony and the whole office has a party to celebrate. We end up drunk and happy, doing karaoke with Megan, celebrating this new chapter of my life as it unfolds in front of us. I feel simultaneously like a kid and a woman, entering the world from a new view. I always thought this moment would terrify me. But having Sound Connections and Alec by my side makes everything feel just a little less intimidating in the end.

Alec and I decide that we don't want to get married right away—we want to spend time being engaged, learning each other, figuring out how we work as a couple and as business partners. It's a decision that makes me feel like we've already grown together. There are no unspoken moments, no doubts, no second guesses—we're meant to be together because we understand each other. And now we're in each other's lives for good, growing and changing, learning how to care for one another in the best way that we know how.

With the money raised and a good chunk of Alec's own earnings contributed, we finally have the funds to start construction on the music wing at Malibu High school. We spend part of the week working in the office, crafting new playlists and sharing success stories from couples who met through the app, while visiting the building site toward the end of the week to make sure that everything is going smoothly. It's a long process, one that stretches for weeks and weeks as Alec crunches numbers and ensures that the funds we raise and the money he contributes is all used to make the building as incredible as it can possibly be. But it's worth it—every time we visit, the place looks even more incredible.

It comes together quickly—studs become insulated, walls painted, rooms constructed, floors laid down, lights installed, doors hung on their hinges. In the meantime, we source instruments and make plans. This will be the guitar room. This will be the orchestral pit. This will house the marching band with every drum and trumpet and trombone they could ever ask for. This will be the dance studio, with mirrors lining every wall, barres installed for practice and stretching.

After months of work, it's finally becoming a nearly usable space. The hall is a sweeping building with high ceilings, great acoustics, and a gorgeous interior. There's even a performance center with rows and rows of comfortable seats along with a detailed stage, ready to host music, dance, and theater. Malibu High School has been transformed. All I can think about as we do a final walkthrough in the building is the kids whose dreams will come to life here.

"It's beautiful," I say to Alec and Mr. Johnston as the three of us explore the building. In just a few weeks it will be open for use by the students. I can already picture them here, instruments in hand, voices loud and happy.

"It's better than anything I could have ever dreamed about," Mr. Johnston says wistfully. We enter the performance hall and he tilts his head back to take in the velvet curtains that frame the stage. "You both have to come for our first performance. In fact, you should come to every performance—I'll get you a special season pass."

Alec laughs. His eyes are bright and full of joy. This man who used to seem so cold and intimidating is now a shining light among all the things that he made possible. Just looking at him makes my heart thump hard in my chest. I reach for his hand and squeeze it in mine, tugging him closer to me, needing to feel him against my side.

"We'd love to come," Alec says. "I want the opportunity to watch these kids blossom, you know?"

"Of course you do," Mr. Johnston says happily. "It's a life changing experience, Alec. That's what I got to do with you, anyway."

If Alec were the kind of man to blush, he'd be bright red right now. But instead he just shakes his head, grinning. "I wouldn't be here right now if it wasn't for you, Mr. Johnston. And I'm sure the kids who will be performing here can say the same."

I see the emotion rise in Mr. Johnston's face. "Would you like a moment to take it in alone?" I ask him, and he nods, his eyes misty.

Alec and I step outside of the building, taking in the cool weather and the breeze whistling through the palm trees. This time next year, school will be back in session. Students will come pouring through those doors and will find themselves standing in front of the hall that we built for them. Inside, they'll find more opportunities than they thought possible for themselves—days full of music, of laughter, of dancing and joy. They'll build talents and find their lives changed because of them. Jobs, internships, even scholarships might open up for them.

And that gives me an idea—I turn to Alec, a smile on my face. He looks down at me with shining eyes.

"I know what we can raise money for next," I say with excitement.

"Oh, do you now? I'm starting to think that you just like spending money," he answers teasingly, a hand cupping my cheek. His skin is so warm against mine.

"It's important," I say, smiling. "Picture this—the kids spend their time here preparing for college. But what happens next? What if they don't have the funds to go and all that talent goes to waste?"

My hands wave in front of me as I talk. Alec watches me with warmth in his eyes. "Scholarships, babe. We could build a fund that sends these kids to school. It might not be much at first, but if we were able to provide a path for them, they'd really be able to focus on their passions. And we could set up internships at Sound Connections, and maybe even Songbird if we manage to annoy Torres enough to make it happen."

Alec laughs, the sound blooming from deep inside of him. "I like the way you think, honey," he says, and then he leans in to kiss me, stealing the breath from my chest, pulling me into him, opening me up to him. "I think it's an amazing idea," he says at last when we pull apart. "I give it the green light. Talk to Megan—you know she'll be thrilled."

I rest my head against his chest and we turn back to the building, standing proud behind us. I wonder what Mr. Johnston is doing inside—if he's overwhelmed by the beauty and potential of it all, just as I was after the first time I saw it nearly completed.

"How do you feel about a fall wedding?" I ask Alec. He strokes my hair with a strong hand, the other pressing me closer to him.

"Hmm, I think it sounds compelling," he answers. "What makes you want a fall wedding?"

"The weather would be so nice," I say dreamily. "Just the right amount of breeze, everyone dancing to stay warm as the sun goes down, pumpkins and spice and all different shades of orange and red and gold!"

"It does sound pretty great when you put it that way," he says, chuckling.

"I think I know a nice venue, too," I add. His laugh vibrates through his chest against my cheek.

"Do you now?"

"The Botanical Gardens," I say softly. "Wouldn't it be perfect to go back to the place where we began?"

He looks down at me, his sea-toned eyes so soft on me, his mouth curled into a satisfied smirk. "I think that could be arranged," he says. "Come on—we need to find Mr. Johnston and say goodbye. We have dinner with your parents soon."

We find Mr. Johnston in the main hall and he shakes hands with Alec, gratitude written all over his face. They smile at each other, two men who have watched each other grow and change over time and are proud of the people that they've become. And then Alec and I make our way out to the car, smiles on our faces, fingers intertwined.

"I can't wait to call you my wife," Alec says from the driver's seat. He hasn't let go of my hand yet. I feel so safe with him there beside me, ready to take on the world.

"Same here, husband," I say with a grin. We pull up to a stoplight and he leans across the center console to kiss me as hard as he can. When the light turns green and someone behind us honks their horn, he pulls away with a laugh.

"I'm so lucky," he says, speeding away into the evening. "I get to kiss a beautiful woman every day for the rest of my life."

I feel the emotion soar in my chest. I feel my life taking flight, my joy so bright that it could power the world, shine as strong as stars overhead in the night.

"Here's to forever, baby," I say, squeezing his hand hard.

He smiles at me and squeezes back.

*****

# Don't miss out!

Visit the website below and you can sign up to receive emails whenever Erica Frost publishes a new book. There's no charge and no obligation.

https://books2read.com/r/B-A-YRSV-AVWHC

**BOOKS 2 READ**

Connecting independent readers to independent writers.

# Also by Erica Frost

Seduced By A Billionaire
Dark Secrets
A Billionaire's Game
Power Play
Ruthless Rival
Taming The Billionaire
The Hated Billionaire
3-Pointer